The Sacrifice

Short stories - volume I

Indrajit GARAI

Copyright © 2016 by Indrajit GARAI

LOC Copyright Registration Number : TX0008673918

All rights reserved by the author

Published by Indrajit GARAI, August 2016

The stories in this book are works of fiction. The names, characters, and events portrayed in these stories are the results of author's imagination alone. Any eventual resemblances to actual persons (living or dead), incidents, and localities are entirely accidental and involuntary.

For Mylène and Estelle

Table of Contents

The Move 5

The Listener 74

The Sacrifice 141

The Move

Guillaume heard the spatter of raindrops on the roof and then the drippings on the floor of the living room. The storm had displaced the tarpaulin again last night. The roof needed to be fixed before autumn, but he didn't see where the money would come from.

There is a limit to what a man can do.

He left a bucket under the stream of droplets and started wiping the floor.

The rain stopped. Guillaume arranged breakfast for Hugo on the dining table, then went out to see how Belinda was doing.

Mustang appeared before the cowshed wagging his tail. Guillaume stooped and rubbed him behind the ears. The dog looked up and yowled. Across the national highway, clouds sailed low over the conifers and alternated their colors in the rising sun. From behind the forest, the highest peak cast a shadow that reached the gate of his farm.

The rooster cried out but stopped abruptly. Mustang perked his ears, sniffed the air, and went on stiff legs toward the henhouse.

Hugo was right. The badger had been making its rounds near the henhouse again, but it stood little chance against Mustang. The dog had the cunning of a Border Collie from his mother; the courage and force of a Malamute from his father; and an instinct that was entirely of his own. With the falling price of milk, Guillaume didn't know what would happen to his farm, but one thing he was absolutely sure of.

For security, he could count on Mustang.

Guillaume entered the cowshed and turned on the lights. The cows stirred then moved toward the milking area. He entered the enclosure of Belinda and checked her temperature—the fever had fallen over the night. From the other side, Old Billy grated his horns on the slats; he wanted to be let in the enclosure with Belinda.

Poor Billy still hadn't adjusted to his solitude, since all his nanny goats were sold. Guillaume couldn't have done any other way; he had to downsize his farm.

The cows were shoving each other at the milking area. Their udders were bursting with milk. Guillaume let Old Billy in Belinda's enclosure, then went toward the cows. He washed the udder of the first cow in the line, checked its nipples for infection, and engaged the milking machine on them.

By the time he finished milking and came out, a half rainbow had risen from the overpass and bent over the chain of Alps. He went back into the cowshed. Hugo was still in the enclosure of the calves, talking to them and feeding them fresh warm milk. The boy never missed a chore.

Guillaume worried sometimes: a boy of Hugo's age should play more with other boys than working in a farm. Maybe, that's why, his son wasn't tough enough.

What could Guillaume do?

Nothing.

He didn't have the money to hire a helping hand. He couldn't marry another woman just to help him on his farm. Outside, Mustang barked and ran toward the gate. A vehicle's tires crunched on the gravels.

Anaïs came out holding a covered platter in her hand.

Guillaume wished her husband came here more often than her, but then Hugo always preferred Anaïs over Joaquin. Guillaume still hadn't figured out why; maybe the boy lacked feminine presence on his farm.

"Where's Hugo?" Anaïs said.

Guillaume called Hugo over. Anaïs gave the platter to the boy and asked him to put it in the fridge.

"What is it again?" Guillaume said.

Anaïs ignored the question. She shouted: "Hugo, are you ready?"

Hugo came running out with his schoolbag and stopped. "Is Louis still sick?"

Guillaume stiffened. But then, Anaïs didn't always talk about Louis to him—unless, it was something serious.

"No." Anaïs turned to go. "We'll pick him up on the

way."

"Look, I've been thinking." Guillaume walked behind her. "You should really stop feeding us."

Anaïs kept walking. "Don't you have other things to think about?"

"Is Joaquin home?"

"No, he is at the strike."

Guillaume stopped. "Which strike?"

Anaïs entered the car and closed the door.

Guillaume reached the car and bent over her window. "Isn't there an anti-strike clause in his contract?"

"Try telling him that."

Anaïs backed up and drove away with Hugo.

Guillaume stood there until her car left the mud trail and turned on the highway. He couldn't decide how to feel about Anaïs this morning, but he was worried about her husband.

Joaquin didn't sell his milk to the regional cooperative of farmers; he sold it to one of the biggest industrial dairy groups in the country. True, Joaquin was a much bigger farmer than him, but that industrial group had the legal artilleries to wipe out Joaquin if he broke their contract.

Guillaume didn't want that disaster for Joaquin's family. In spite of all his tensions with Anaïs, Joaquin had been kind to him.

Besides, there was Louis too.

He needed to dissuade Joaquin from the strike.

He called Mustang over and went into the cowshed. Belinda was on her feet now, giving a thorough lick to Old Billy, who opened his eyes barely to look at Mustang, and then went back to nodding his head. Guillaume unlocked the double doors and let Mustang take the cows to the pasture.

He returned to Belinda and Old Billy. He led them out of the cowshed, into the enclosure behind the house. The farm cat, chasing a mouse on the patch of grass, promptly moved out of the range of Old Billy's horns. Guillaume closed the gate of the enclosure and returned to the cowshed. He started to clean up the place and refurnish it with fresh straws.

He pondered how he could dissuade Joaquin from the strike, without getting too involved with his family.

Even though Joaquin never showed any signs of jealousy, Guillaume didn't want to come too close to Anaïs. She had made her choice back then, and she still kept doing everything according to her own will.

At times, Guillaume thought he should move out to a different region altogether and start all over. True, he could never be absolutely sure about Louis. But then, Joaquin was doing a decent job in holding the rein of his family; without Guillaume around, he certainly would feel more secure with Anaïs and do better.

But the problem was: Louis had become Hugo's best friend.

Hugo's mother never came. Guillaume couldn't understand her, but he had learned to pardon her for that. His own parents did everything they could do to help Hugo—until the avalanche killed them two years ago, and the boy lost everyone who cared for him.

Well, not exactly. People in this village loved Hugo. Particularly, his former colleagues at the Gendarmerie of the Alps; every time they met Hugo, they pushed him to become a gendarme like them.

For Guillaume, the boy was too fragile and sensitive to become a gendarme.

That was the main reason why Guillaume had decided not to leave this village. An unknown place, with its unknown people, would be too hard for Hugo to deal with right now.

When Guillaume came out of the cattle shed, the July sun was at its zenith over the lake. The air felt sticky, humid, and hot. He showered, ate breakfast, then loaded the refrigerated milk on his trailer and left the farm. The highway was jammed with tourist cars and motor-homes, going to the new vacation centers that were raised almost overnight in the places of the old farms.

He was glad his buyer was not an industrial but a cooperative.

True, not many farmers took active role in the day-to-day management of their cooperative—that's why they had to hire an external management company last year—but, overall, even if the payments for their milk often came in late, the cooperative did a good job in looking after the interest of the farmers.

At least, so far.

Two miles down, he took the exit to his cooperative and pulled into their service station for collecting milk. After the sanitary tests were run and the milk transferred, Guillaume went to see the director.

"Have a seat, Guillaume. What can I do for you?"

"Those accounts in arrears need to be settled." He could get by with his old clothes and shoes, but not his son.

"I know, I know."

"Have our distributors paid?"

The director pointed his thumb downward. "We're losing ground since Europe announced elimination of quotas."

"Isn't that good news for us?"

"No. We're more expensive than our neighbors."

Guillaume didn't know how the farmers in the neighboring countries survived, but, for him, the market price of milk was already eight cents below his cost of production per liter. And he was not the only farmer in the Alps with that problem.

Since he took over this farm from his father, at least four hundred farms had closed their doors. Some sold their cattle to the mega farms in the north; others put theirs to sleep. Those who couldn't bear the grief and the humiliation chose to end their lives too. On the tombs of their farms, rich retirees built their luxurious chalets, with private saunas and swimming pools overlooking the lake. The municipalities favored them because they brought more jobs to the area, more fees in transactions, and more tax money than the staggering, emaciated farms.

Guillaume had already downsized his farm twice. He had retained only the seventy-two best of his cows, and was just breaking even with the regional subsidy. The market deregulation could drive down the price of milk further, which would bring catastrophe on his farm and others.

"What's happening to the cooperative's profits?"

The director frowned. "You mean from last year?"

"Right. When will those be distributed to the farmers?"

"The governing committee decided to retain that profit."

"Why?"

"The cooperative needs to grow."

"Where will the cooperative be without the farmers?"

"Guillaume." The director rose from his seat. "I know

how you feel, but the process is not that simple."

"I want to speak to that governing committee."

"Why don't you start considering an alternative buyer?"

Guillaume glared at the director.

But the director's face showed no hostility; rather, his eyes pleaded. Guillaume couldn't figure out what the director was trying to say.

The truth was: he had no alternative buyer really. He could sell his milk to the industrials, but then he would have the same problems as Joaquin. He could stop selling milk and start making cheese, but he couldn't do all that alone *and* keep running his household. That's why, when he downsized his farm, he sold those cheese-making equipments.

He could sell his cattle and start working for someone, but that would be an outright insult toward his late parents.

There had to be a way to survive with dignity without selling the farm.

The director said he would file a petition with the governing committee on behalf of the farmers. He started saying how important it was to keep calm during the price war, but Guillaume wasn't listening anymore. He had issues he could do something about, rather than blaming others or complaining about the system. He thanked the director and left.

The roof needed to be repaired before the next storm brought it down.

There were talks of riots and barricades around the village. Which meant the industrials had pushed the farmers to the point where they saw they could no longer survive by stealing each other's business; they had to stand shoulder to shoulder, advance together, and push the industrials back. Finally, the farmers had put on the red cap of liberty, and were ready to revolt.

Guillaume didn't like violence.

At the same time, he could see the point of his fellow farmers when they said this was how changes had always happened in France. Neither the public nor the government reacted until the sufferings were pushed to the extreme. Then the revolt occurred, and everything went upside down.

Not without a cost. And the public paid for it.

It was this reactive action—as opposed to the proactive prevention—that depressed Guillaume.

Several times in the past, he tried to organize the farmers, make them see that one man's loss was not another man's gain but a collective loss for all. The farmers listened to his rhetoric, and then went back to doing exactly what they had been doing before. More popular Guillaume became in his commune, more he saw how powerless he was in such matters.

The only thing he had some control over was this: save his own farm, without hurting others.

Last week, he found out their cooperative was no longer serving the farmers' interest at its best; the management company had its own interest to serve first. But, that too was beyond his control.

He swam to the center of the lake and floated on his back. The early afternoon sky—framed by the firs, the spruces, and the distant peaks—seemed bottomless and free of worries. This was where he used to come with Anaïs after school, to escape the pettiness of their village. All that changed when he joined the Rescue Squad of the gendarmerie, and Anaïs chose Joaquin over him.

Guillaume could understand her: life wasn't secure with a rescuer in the Alps.

He heard the soft splashing and straightened himself. Mustang was swimming out to him as usual. The dog always kept an eye on them from the pasture; he never missed an occasion to swim with Guillaume. He was glad Mustang didn't let Hugo go near the water alone.

Guillaume reached out and patted the dog on his head. Then he saw the car of Anaïs parked by the road above the beach.

She stood knee deep in water, with the top of her bikini off. She probably couldn't recognize him from there, but she must have seen Mustang swimming toward him. No other dog in the village swam like that.

She lifted her arms above the head and started tying her hair.

Guillaume averted his eyes. He hated what that sight of her was doing to him.

If he had resisted her the night before her wedding, he wouldn't be living in doubts about Louis today. She didn't change much after her wedding. If he could understand her motives clearly, he could put a label on her and move on, but her actions always had a double meaning.

One thing he was sure about her: she was still dangerous for him. He needed to stay out of her life as much as possible.

He swam to the other end of the lake and jogged home with Mustang. There were purchases to make from the neighboring town.

Guillaume parked his truck near the town's square and walked toward the store that supplied his farm. A woman, dressed in fluorescent jacket, approached him and handed out a flier.

"Monsieur, I'm doing survey for a cooperative." She raised a notepad. "Do you have a few minutes?"

Guillaume didn't, but his cooperative's name was on her flier. "Sure. What's the survey about?"

"Do you know that a big French dairy group has opened a factory in Southeast Asia?"

"No, I didn't." The French industrials could do their business wherever they wanted.

"Do you know that the same dairy group has signed a contract with the largest farm in Southeast Asia? A farm that holds more than six hundred thousand cows in absolutely horrible conditions."

"Wait, Mademoiselle." Guillaume stepped back. "If you're testing me on how French industrials do their business abroad, then you've picked the wrong person."

The woman narrowed her eyes. "Monsieur, do you have a young child?"

"Yes, I do."

"Do you know the same group sells dairy products in this town that your child eats three times a day?"

Hugo drank milk from his cows only, ate cheese and yogurts that Anaïs made at her farm. "I see your point, Mademoiselle. But I have little control over where the French industrials choose to buy their milk from."

"Do you know that the Asians have just opened a factory in France, to produce powdered milk for their own consumption?"

"Yes, I do." The farmers were worried the Asian buyers would drive down the price of milk further.

"Do you know the Asians opened this factory *after* a number of their children died from milk contamination?"

"Yes, I know that too." Now he saw where she was heading, and he couldn't help admiring the young woman's skills.

"Let's think. A major French dairy group feeds French children with milk from Asia, whereas the Asians trust French milk more than their own, when it comes to feeding their children. How would you call this situation?"

"Ironic. But, what do you expect the French to do about it?"

"Your child's health—should it be in the hands of those industrials or yours?"

"It has always been in my hands, and it will always be."

She looked disappointed.

"Keep going, Mademoiselle. I'm still listening."

"Will you pay higher price for the milk that comes from here? From cows that are raised with fresh herbs and pure air of our mountains."

"Yes, I will."

Guillaume admired their cooperative's director for his initiative. This surveyor was building excellent consumer awareness. He wondered if the other cooperatives in the Alps had started doing the same.

He didn't want to pretend anymore. "Listen, Mademoiselle. I'm a farmer, and I sell my milk to this cooperative. You've done a great job in inspiring me, and I'm sure you'll do the same with others."

The woman blinked in embarrassment. "Thank you, Monsieur."

"Good luck." He turned away from her. "And give your boss my best regards."

He entered the store but kept pondering over what the surveyor had said. She was right; yet she missed an important point. The issue before urban consumers was not of price only, but also of convenience.

Most could tell the difference between milk from the mountains in France and milk from the mega farms in Southeast Asia; but most also didn't want the inconvenience of having to buy that mountain milk from special distribution channels, because their closest supermarkets refused to stock that milk on their shelves. The farmers of the mountains couldn't survive by selling their milk in the local markets only.

Habits of urban consumers were changing with internet, though.

He had heard that some of them were having their preferred milk delivered directly from the regions to their doors, and they were paying higher price for their choice of quality. He wondered why his cooperative didn't tap into this network. He was going to talk to the director about it.

He finished the purchases and returned to his farm. The encounter with the surveyor had lifted his spirit. He called the director of his cooperative and praised him for his initiative.

"We sent you the money this morning," the director said.

"What's happening with your petition?"

"It's being reviewed in Luxemburg."

"In Luxemburg?"

"That's where the head of our management company is."

That was news to Guillaume.

Their cooperative was now being controlled by an offshore company in Luxemburg. He wasn't sure what that meant for the farmers in his region. Even if he raised the question with the other farmers, he doubted they would have the head to think about it now. And the managers of the cooperative knew that too.

He wondered why the director never mentioned this to him before.

But he wasn't in a mood to discuss this now. There were other issues pressing on his mind. He thanked the director and went out to the yard.

The sun was right above the house. High up, the

eastern wind bent the cirrus clouds in the form of croissants. He had heard there was a depression nearby. From what he saw, the bad weather would be here in two or three days at the max. On the roof, the tarpaulin had displaced again, and now flapped in the wind.

He climbed the roof and tied the tarpaulin back in its place.

He couldn't go on like this for ever. The structure would rot, and the roof would collapse. The repair would cost him more than six thousand euros; he would have to dip into the savings he had kept aside for Hugo.

He came down from the roof. He mixed fodder with dietary complements, trailed the container behind his tractor to the silo, and transferred the mix inside.

He entered the vegetable garden. He picked one lettuce, two cucumbers, a few zucchinis, tomatoes, and peppers for the day. Then he took out the weeds, loosened the earth around the plants, and carried the vegetables to the kitchen.

He ate a quick lunch of omelet and salad, cleaned the house, then sat before his computer and started entering the data of milk production, sanitation checks, and expenses of his farm. His accounts were dangerously close to the red. If payments didn't come in next month on time, he would default on his mortgage again.

One more default after that, and he would be kicked out of his farm.

His father had been prudent and paid off all the debts left by his ancestors. What his father couldn't foresee, however, was the colossal amount of inheritance tax that fell upon Guillaume from the market value of their land, which had multiplied due to the frenzy of constructions around the Alps.

Unlike the other farms in this village, the Farm of Old Billy sat on the southern slope of a picturesque hill, looking over a spruce-lined lake that was created by a retreating glacier two million years ago. The view of the three highest peaks, including the majestic Mont Blanc, added to the market value of his farm. After his father died, Guillaume inherited a land that was priced at seven times higher than what his father had paid. Guillaume had to re-mortgage his farm with a bank, in order to raise the money for inheritance tax.

The real estate builders knew all that too, along with his financial difficulties; the same bank loaned them money to build around here. That's why those builders kept coming to his door for the land, but he wasn't going to sell his farm.

The sun had crossed over the lake, and now stood above the conifers that lined the high pasture. The curtains swayed, and a gush of air came in with smells of compost, flowers, and rain. From the western sky, a high stack of dark gray cumulonimbus clouds hung heavily and blocked the mountain ridge from his view. He turned off his computer, called out for Mustang, and left the house to fetch his cattle.

Hugo was telling Louis how they could build an observation deck on the walnut tree, when Joaquin stamped into the house, red-eyed, and staggered toward the kitchen, ignoring the two boys altogether. Hugo stopped talking.

"Don't know what's happening to Dad," Louis said.

"Why is he drunk again?"

"They quarreled last night."

"About my father?"

Louis lowered his eyes.

Hugo knew how difficult this was for Louis. He wished he could do something about it, but he was too small for that.

Anaïs came in with two steaming chocolates. "Louis, did you tell that boy in your school not to push Hugo around?"

"I can do that myself," Hugo said.

"Let me change your bandage."

Anaïs went out, then returned with her first-aid kit.

"Mom," Louis said. "Is Dad going to the blockade?"

Anaïs frowned. "What blockade?"

"Near the shopping center."

"How do you know there is a blockade?"

"Dad was telling someone on the phone."

Anaïs sighed. She clenched her jaws and went into the kitchen. A hushed, hostile exchange followed. Then Joaquin yelled:

"Stop! I'm doing what any dignified man will do."

"Hauling your cows to the shopping center?" Anaïs sniffed. "That's stupid."

"Is that what Guillaume said?"

"No."

"Did he come over here?"

"He never comes when you are not here."

"That doesn't stop you from going over to his place."

"You just said you're a dignified man."

"Just go and leave me alone."

Anaïs was still fuming when she took Hugo to her car. Hugo wanted Louis to come with them too, but Louis said he would stay home with his dad. Maybe Louis thought he was big enough to stop Joaquin from going to that blockade.

Hugo fastened the seatbelt and looked at Anaïs. "I don't want Louis to keep defending me anymore."

Anaïs pulled out of their driveway, without saying a word.

"I said: I can take care of myself."

Her arms straightened on the steering wheel. "Did your mother call?"

"No."

Anaïs shook her head. "Do you know what I see when I look at you?"

Hugo held his breath.

"The best of Guillaume."

Hugo released his breath: that was exactly what he wanted to hear.

"I'm glad you didn't turn out to be a coward like your mother."

Hugo startled; his face grew hot.

Anaïs glanced at him. "Don't feel sorry for your mother."

"Why did you call my mother a coward?"

"Ask your father about it."

The conversation stopped. Hugo was glad. Anaïs turned on the dirt trail, drove up to his father's tractor, and then opened the door for Hugo. Hugo was relieved to get out of her car today.

Father wasn't there. Hugo didn't feel like doing his chores at the farm right away. He stood there, mulling over what Anaïs had just said.

He had heard the story about his mother from his grandparents, but still he couldn't stop resenting Anaïs for calling her a coward. He wanted to tell his father about this. But, maybe his father still loved his mother, and he would be hurt by hearing it.

Father had a lot on his mind already.

Father seemed angry with Anaïs too. Maybe she did something he didn't like. Maybe she was the coward here, and not his mother.

Anaïs flattered him, though, when she said he looked like his father.

Father was the biggest hero Hugo had ever seen in his life. Now, he wasn't thinking only about his father's physical strength. He was also thinking about those other qualities that go with a hero.

Humility, for example.

Hugo had seen other strong men in their entourage, particularly those rescuers from his father's gendarmerie, but none had the ability of his father to push back the women who fell upon them.

Maybe Anaïs, like one of those women, desired his father secretly.

Maybe that's why she was so jealous of his mother. Sometimes, he had caught Anaïs looking strangely at his father; he couldn't figure out what was on her mind. He couldn't understand why she was so sweet with him and so rough with his father.

But then, didn't Hugo, himself, behave the same way, when he wanted something badly, but he couldn't have it?

The thought made him smile.

Father was so much better than Joaquin. Hugo had seen Joaquin ogling at other women, even when Anaïs was around. He could understand why, having a husband like Joaquin, Anaïs could admire a man like his father. He felt bad for Anaïs that his father was so cold and distant toward her. But then, she might have hurt his father in some way that he didn't know.

He would never know. Father never talked about Anaïs in his presence.

All Hugo knew was: Anaïs had cared for him since Grandmother passed away.

He couldn't dislike Anaïs for liking his father. He couldn't hold on to hurt feelings toward his best friend's mother. He was going to pardon Anaïs for calling his mother a coward.

Now he felt like doing his chores.

One thing he was sure of: he wanted to grow up to be a man like Father.

He was going to work as a rescuer at the same gendarmerie as his father. And he was going to keep tending this farm with as much care as his father gave now. He put two fingers in his mouth and whistled for Mustang.

Old Billy replied from the arena behind the house.

That's right! In his war of thoughts, he had completely forgotten about his session with Old Billy.

Hugo collected the eggs from the henhouse, fed the chickens, then took off his shirt and entered the arena. Old Billy stood ready for him. Belinda moved to one side and watched Hugo intensely, as he went around Old Billy looking for a place to grab.

Old Billy never gave up a chance to fight. It was certainly exciting for Belinda to watch the fight, but she never failed to intervene when one fighter went too far out of his limit. Old Billy's horns were as deadly as the blades of the tractor; but, like Hugo, Belinda certainly knew that these sparring sessions were indispensable to make Hugo the best rescuer in the gendarmerie. Like Hugo, she also knew that the training went better when Mustang didn't stand at Hugo's side, growling at Old Billy.

Old Billy always reared up on his hind legs and charged at Hugo.

But then, Old Billy always missed Hugo too, and landed at his side. He stayed there just long enough so Hugo could grab him around the neck, wrestle him to the ground, and hold him down there. Then the process started all over again and continued in rounds, until Hugo tired himself out and lay flat on the ground. At that point, Belinda came and licked Hugo from head to feet, as if he had won the toughest wrestling match in the world and needed all the cares to recover.

Belinda's rough tongue healed Hugo. Old Billy never protested against this display of affection. Once the sparring and the licking sessions were over, he carried Hugo the Winner on his back around the arena, while Hugo waved at the invisible crowd applauding him for his victory.

But, these days, Old Billy was losing his battles too quickly.

And his back sagged more and more, when he carried Hugo around the arena.

At first, Hugo thought Old Billy was sick. But then, his father explained that senility was coming over Old Billy, since the nanny goats were taken away from him. Even those other farmers, who used to bring their goats to Old Billy, sold their beasts too. For over a year now, Old Billy had been out of work, and was losing his place in this world quickly. Only Hugo's sparring and Belinda's licking kept him going.

Hugo would have liked Mustang to spar with Old Billy too, but the dog never trusted him with his horns.

Hugo descended from Old Billy's back and rubbed his horns. The animal's eyes opened wider. Only for a second, Hugo saw the same flash in his pupils that he used to have when he charged at an unruly goat on the high pasture, where they took their cattle in the summer.

When Hugo was younger, his grandfather explained one night how one of the nanny goats had eloped with a male ibex from the sheer cliffs near the high pasture, and how Young Billy came into being after that.

Those horns that Old Billy had inherited from his ibex father were the biggest treasures he had. Even today, well beyond his prime, Old Billy still felt proud when someone appreciated his horns.

Hugo heard Mustang before he saw him coming.

Father was returning with the cattle, and Mustang was impatient to get the herd into the shed; he was late for his squirrel hunt in the forest with Hugo. Father froze when he saw Belinda licking Hugo on the back; the same blank look came over his face. Then he shook his head and followed the cattle into the shed.

That look of Father always puzzled Hugo.

Belinda's licking felt so good, and he couldn't understand why that made Father so sad. Maybe Father had a cow too, who licked him when he was young, and Belinda reminded him of that cow. As adult, he still wanted to be licked probably, but he was too ashamed to have it done.

Suddenly, in the eyes of his mind, Hugo saw Father being licked by a cow.

The licking made Father giggle, and Hugo couldn't stop giggling either.

All Father had to do was: stop being so serious and behave like a child. Then Belinda would lick him whenever he wanted. She didn't have a calf for god knows how long, but Hugo was glad Father kept her on the farm.

She was important for Old Billy.

Hugo put on his shirt, whistled for Mustang, and ran out of the arena. The dog was already on the hill outside their house, with his ears perked and tongue hanging.

Guillaume drove into the town square with Hugo where the festival was being held. In the wake of the price war and the controversies around the new resort, the place was packed with people this evening. Guillaume held Hugo by the hand and walked toward the church. Music was being played on the stage, and people strolled among the sizzles and smokes that rose from the barbecue stands.

Anaïs was there too, with Louis.

She looked worried. She came over and kissed Guillaume on the cheeks, and he didn't need to ask her where Joaquin was. He left Hugo with them at the barbecue stand and went to speak with his former colleagues from the gendarmerie.

They were discussing how the vacation center for low income families was going to be demolished, and, in its place, a luxurious resort would be built, when the Swiss woman who had purchased the site stepped toward them and greeted Guillaume. The gendarmes moved away.

"Do you remember giving me ski lessons?" The Swiss woman canted her head and rounded her lips.

"No, I don't." He worked as ski instructor a decade ago.

She straightened her head and narrowed her eyes to a half-squint, but Guillaume had become immune to those gestures from women. He glanced at his former colleagues. They were watching him and the Swiss woman discreetly, with a mix of amusement and disdain on their faces.

Guillaume looked at his watch. "What can I do for you, Ma'am?"

"We need someone to run the sports facilities in the resort."

"If I think of someone, I'll let you know."

Her mouth curved downward. "You can't do it?"

"I have my own farm to run."

"We can talk about a financial package for your farm."

"No, Ma'am. I won't close my farm."

"Do you know how much—"

"Yes, I know the value of my land." He couldn't help clenching his jaws. "I still want to keep my farm."

"Alright. If you ever change your—"

"I won't change my mind. You have a nice evening, Ma'am."

The Swiss woman left. Guillaume's former boss came

over, with two full plates of food.

"Your blue eyes and deep tan hemorrhage the hearts of women." The Chief handed one plate to Guillaume. "How long are you planning to remain a saint?"

"She asked me to close my farm and work for her."

"Ski instructor? Or, mountain guide?" The Chief winked. "She offered you a great salary I suppose."

"Right." Guillaume blew. "When the next world war breaks out, and all those tourists stop coming to France, how am I going to feed my son?"

"How are you feeding him now?"

"Hugo isn't starving."

"You know we still miss you in the squad." The Chief widened his stance. "We can't match that Swiss woman's salary exactly, but our salaries are steady and sure. And we get by with dignity."

"I know." If he ever had to look for work, he would certainly choose the squad over her resort. "But I'm doing what I have to do."

"You're speaking like the old man I knew."

They chatted about how Guillaume's father was a great rescuer too; about how more and more tourists were skiing hors piste irresponsibly, putting themselves and the rescue workers in peril. Then Guillaume took leave from the gendarmes and went to see the farmers he knew.

The director of his cooperative was talking to a group of bakers, butchers, and sellers of fruits and vegetables. He was encouraging them to collaborate with the local farmers to sell their milk and dairy products. He saw Guillaume and came over with a wry smile.

"I'm leaving the cooperative."

Guillaume froze. "When?"

"End of this month."

"Are you resigning?"

"Not voluntarily."

The petition the director had filed on behalf of the farmers had to do something with his forced resignation. Guillaume realized he was grinding his teeth, but the issue was beyond his control. He didn't choose that management company alone.

"So, what are you doing from next month?" Guillaume knew the director had two kids and a wife to feed.

"Moving to Jura."

"Why Jura?"

"Farmers there are building an alternative cooperative."

"Alternative?"

"I mean the way a cooperative should really be run."

"Can we not do that here?"

"I've tested the water already. The municipality here

won't make it easy for us."

"Why?"

"The same folks in Luxemburg send the real estate builders here."

Uh-huh. "Jura doesn't have this problem?"

"No. The building craze hasn't picked up there yet."

"Alright." Anaïs was running toward them with the mobile phone stuck to her ear, and Guillaume didn't like the look on her face. "I wish you all the best in Jura then."

"We'll keep in touch."

Anaïs handed her phone to Guillaume. "Police picked up Joaquin."

The leader of the blockade explained to Guillaume that the manifestation near the shopping center had derailed a little. An eighteen-wheeler that belonged to the industrial had been overturned, and the vehicle was in flame.

Guillaume handed the phone back to Anaïs and ran to his truck.

In the last two weeks, the air had chilled significantly. The trajectory of the late September sun was still high in the sky, but, this afternoon, the stratus clouds were breaking up and forming cumulus over the northeast ridge. Guillaume picked some apples and figs and pears for the week, then entered the vegetable garden.

Rain had ruined quite a bit of the vegetables.

He recovered what he could, then took the rest to the compost. He returned with a trowel and loosened the earth around the remaining plants.

The celeries, the turnips, and the black radishes were growing fine, but the cabbages had drawn some insects. He moved the pots of basils near them. The weather was cooling fast; there could be frost in a week or two. He brought plastic sheets and stakes from the tool-shed, and started building a low greenhouse over the rows of vegetables.

The skin of the onions was thicker this year. The furs were denser on the animals too. The squirrels collected more nuts than usual. And the groundhogs had grown fatter this autumn.

All this meant: a harsher and longer winter this year.

Hugo had grown out of his winter coat and shoes; Guillaume would need to replace them by the end of next month. The falling price of milk wasn't going to help him in those purchases.

Nor would the inflating costs and the rising taxes.

While incomes of public kept falling, most businesses used the argument of recession to hike their prices; and the government used the argument of deficits to raise their taxes. Even the traffic authorities went around more aggressively, searching for the slightest infractions and slapping the drivers with huge fines. The battle for survival had pushed everyone beyond the realm of reasons.

Guillaume saw his hands had stopped working.

He had no control over these issues, but thinking about them had stopped him from doing what he did have some control over. The garden needed to be tended properly; the roof needed to be fixed quickly. The impotent thoughts, like the ones he had been thinking, always veiled his mind with a haze and altered his judgment on critical issues he could do something about. He finished building the greenhouse while fighting his resentments, and then went out of the garden.

He climbed the roof. He removed the tarpaulin and started reinforcing the slats of the structure. He heard crunches of tires on the gravel then saw Anaïs's car entering the yard. He stopped. It wasn't the end of school day yet; there was no reason for her to come here at this hour.

He was thinking about how to make her go away, when Joaquin opened the door and rolled out of the car. Guillaume heaved a sigh of relief.

But then, what was Joaquin doing here with Anaïs's car?

Something must have happened to her.

Guillaume left what he was doing and scurried down the ladder.

Joaquin was at the back of the house, looking at the

stacks of shingles. He said, "I hope these didn't wipe you out."

"Almost. What can I do for you?"

"I came here to give you a hand with the shingles."

Guillaume couldn't believe his ears. He hoped Anaïs didn't watch him from her porch with a pair of binocular. He didn't need help with the shingles really, but then he couldn't find a decent excuse to turn Joaquin away either.

They climbed the roof together.

"How did it go at the court?" Guillaume knew Joaquin had appealed against his fine.

"The right to strike is in the constitution."

"Will they make you pay the seventeen thousand euros?"

Joaquin shrugged. "The question is: can I? Life doesn't seem worth living anymore."

His tone shocked Guillaume. "Why don't you change buyer?"

"To your cooperative, for example?" Joaquin sniffled.

Joaquin was right. After the director left, Guillaume's cooperative aligned price with the industrials. Other cooperatives in the region were doing the same.

"I entered the dairy futures market," Joaquin said.

Guillaume stopped pecking the nail. "Why?"

"The price of milk is falling, and I need the guarantee."

"But, you'll lose money if the price rises."

"The price will never rise."

"Are you sure?"

"Absolutely."

Guillaume wasn't so sure.

True, ending of quotas had glutted the market, but there were seasonal factors that could still raise the price of milk. For example: the fall of supply after the spring; or, the rise of demand after the autumn.

Then there were other risks that could hike price unexpectedly.

A broker from Paris had called Guillaume too about those futures contracts. He trusted neither the broker nor his contracts. From what little he understood, those futures looked like financial time bombs to him.

He tried to convince Joaquin to get out of those futures, but Joaquin wouldn't listen to him.

Weeks passed. Joaquin kept offsetting his losses from falling price by his gains from futures, while Guillaume kept barely afloat with his farm.

Then, one night late October, Guillaume's phone rang frantically. Anaïs said their cows were seriously ill from fodder contamination, and Joaquin had lost his head. Guillaume jumped into his pickup truck and drove to their farm.

The veterinarian was there, running wildly among the beasts that groaned on the ground and plunging his syringe into their flesh, while Anaïs and Louis held Joaquin at a corner. Six cows had died already. Others had their bellies swollen and mouths foaming. Guillaume took a syringe and joined the doctor.

By the light of the dawn, most of Joaquin's cattle perished.

What was thought to be fodder contamination actually turned out to be an epidemic. The region lost two thirds of its cows. Guillaume lost seventeen. Price of milk climbed sharply. The open futures burned Joaquin's account and drove him into bankruptcy. The bank closed his credit lines, and the court started seizing the assets of his farm.

Then, one afternoon, Hugo came running back from school, wide-eyed and disoriented.

Guillaume left what he was doing and picked Hugo up in his arms.

But Hugo could barely speak. Guillaume gathered from the boy's disjointed words that there had been a serious accident on Joaquin's farm, and Anaïs had fainted in their home. He asked Hugo to stay at the farm and speared out with his pickup truck.

He saw the ambulance and the police cars long before

he reached Joaquin's farm. Their pasture had been taped out by the police. At the far corner, where the river bent around the pasture, the paramedics were lifting a body from the field and placing it on a stretcher. The body was covered from head to feet in white, with red blotches all over the sheet. Two policemen stood at the edge of the river, talking into their radios.

Guillaume stopped the engine and sprang out of the truck.

On their porch, he heard how the tractor had run over Joaquin, crushed his head, and then gone into the river. Louis was in the living room, with his hand stuck in the mouth. Guillaume lifted him off the ground, but the boy shook his head and pointed in the direction of the kitchen.

Anaïs stood leaning over the counter, frozen like a statue of glass.

She said, in a measured tone, that the bailiff had come to their home the day before. This morning, Joaquin had been leafing through his life insurance contract and talking to someone on the phone about how to delay the seizure of their farm by the court. She handed Guillaume a page from the life insurance contract.

A clause was underlined in ink: it excluded any payoff in case of suicide, if committed within two years from the date of signing.

But Joaquin had signed his contract eleven and a half years ago, right after he married Anaïs. That clause was invalid in his case, and the insurance company would have to pay.

Guillaume gave her back the paper and lowered his head.

Mid November, the market cut the price of milk by six more cents. For Guillaume, the price now fell eighteen cents below his cost of production. Even with the subsidies from the region, he could no longer go on feeding his cows and paying the other expenses of his farm.

The bank saw this as an opportunity and offered him a loan at high interest rate.

But Guillaume didn't see any point in running a business that kept him sinking in debt everyday rather than pulling him out. Other farmers sold their cattle or put them to sleep, but Guillaume couldn't imagine ending the lives of his cows that he and his father had raised with so many years of work.

He thought for days what he could sell to reimburse some of his debt and reduce the interest charges on his farm, but he couldn't find anything he could dispose off and still keep running his operations.

Finally, he sold his cattle to a reasonable farm on the plane.

They came with their trucks. While Mustang barked and growled at them, they loaded his cows one by one into their vehicles.

Except for Belinda.

That was fine with Guillaume because she was important for Hugo.

Mustang chased the trucks till they turned on the highway, and then howled for days and nights. Belinda watched the dog with tears in her eyes. Even Old Billy didn't aim his horns at the dog after that.

Little by little, Hugo managed to calm Mustang down. But, without the cattle to look after, the dog never found his place back in the farm.

With the twenty percent down-payment that the buyer made to Guillaume, he paid off his mortgage charges in arrears and the temporary credits extended to him by his suppliers. The balance from the sell of his cattle would be paid to him in two weeks, after all the verifications were made—that was the usual practice in such transactions. He was happy he didn't have to sell his cattle to a mega farm in the north that packed several thousand cows under the same roof.

He didn't need the pasture, the cowshed, and the tractor anymore. He could sell those too and use the proceeds, along with the balance of payment from his cattle, to pay off the rest of the debt with the bank. He would still be left with some savings, which he could use until he found a job at the gendarmerie again.

And he could keep living on his farm!

Most of it qualified as agricultural land, so the property tax wasn't exorbitant. His family had lived here for generations, and Hugo was born here too. Even if he wanted, he couldn't move out to a cheaper place in the village—not many neighbors would accept tenants like Belinda, Old Billy, and Mustang.

One evening, when he was helping Hugo with his homework, his mobile phone rang. It was the ex-director of his cooperative; he had heard from Jura about the fate of Guillaume's cattle. They exchanged briefly about their new lives, and then the ex-director's tone became serious.

"Listen, I need someone here to run the operations."

Guillaume tensed. "Uh-huh."

"How do you feel about moving over to Jura?"

"I can't."

"I guess it has to do with Hugo."

"He has all his friends here." Besides, he couldn't imagine hauling Mustang, Belinda, and Old Billy to another part of France. Nor could he imagine Hugo without these animals.

"I know. It's not easy for my kids here either."

"Thanks for the offer, though."

"Call me, if you ever need it."

"I will."

"Best of luck."

December came and went, but Guillaume still didn't receive the balance of payment from the sell of his cattle. Then the purchasing farm filed for bankruptcy.

Its assets were seized for liquidation, from which the creditors would be paid proportional to their loans, which meant Guillaume would receive only forty percent of what he was supposed to get. And, that too not immediately, but in a year at the earliest.

He had already exchanged contract with a buyer for the sell of his pasture, but the transaction would not complete for another three months. And, given this was not the best part of his land, the proceeds from its sell would not reimburse the remaining part of his debt with the bank.

The money he had collected by selling his tractor kept him barely floating with the mortgage charges and the other expenses of living. The Chief of the gendarmerie tried hard to negotiate with the government a job for Guillaume, but there was hiring freeze at the moment. If anything good came out, the earliest Guillaume could start there would be in summer.

Meanwhile, Belinda grew nervous in the empty cowshed.

Then, one night, she fell in the drinking trough and

injured her shoulder. The antibiotics didn't work; the infected wound turned into gangrene; the veterinarian had to amputate her leg. She lay moaning for days, showed no signs of healing. Finally, Guillaume asked the doctor to put an end to her misery.

Old Billy watched everything from his enclosure.

After Belinda was put to sleep, he refused to eat or rise to his feet. Then, one morning, he stood up and walked briskly around the farm—as if he had overcome his sorrow and recovered his interest in life again. In the afternoon, he even sparred with Hugo.

But, that evening, Mustang grew itchy around Old Billy.

The dog kept sniffing the air around the farm, then pointed its snout at the sky and let out painful howls. His cries sharpened through the night. Guillaume called the veterinarian, and the doctor had to give a tranquilizing shot to the dog. Hugo refused to go to bed after that. Together, they sat by Mustang for the rest of the night.

Next morning, Old Billy never rose from his sleep.

They carried Old Billy to the high pasture and buried him at a corner overlooking the farm. Mustang cried during the burial, then whimpered through the night. They were surprised the dog had such deep feelings for Old Billy, in spite of the number of times he had been thrashed by those horns.

Next morning, they couldn't find Mustang anywhere.

For three full days and nights, with people from the village, Guillaume searched nonstop for Mustang, leaving Hugo with Anaïs and Louis. They didn't find the dog anywhere, alive or dead; not even a trace of his fur.

Guillaume found paw prints on snow of the high pasture, near the grave of Old Billy, but those prints could have come from the wolves that had been reintroduced into the mountains. No one from any of the neighboring villages saw a dog like Mustang anywhere, neither in the mountains nor in the valleys. No tourist reported having seen a lost dog roaming on the ski slopes or on the hiking trails.

Meanwhile, Hugo grew restless.

He stopped eating and sleeping. On the fourth day, when the boy fainted, Anaïs called the pediatrician. The boy had lost one more kilo—in total three, since Belinda and Old Billy died—and that was too much for a kid of his age. They all tried their best to talk Hugo into accepting the loss of Mustang, but the boy refused sternly. Finally, the gendarmerie combed the mountains with a helicopter, but that too led nowhere.

Mustang had simply vanished from this earth.

Yet, Hugo refused to consider the possibility of the dog's death. For him, someone had stolen Mustang.

But, given the dog's vigilance and strength, Guillaume couldn't see how anyone could do that, unless he was drugged into sleep. That too seemed unlikely, because Mustang never accepted food from anyone he didn't know. Even if someone stole him somehow, Guillaume couldn't see how the dog could be kept tamed for so long.

On the sixth day, when Guillaume was taking Hugo to the pediatrician again, his home telephone rang. It was the commissariat of police calling, from a town about one hundred seventy kilometers away from his village. Mustang had injured two skiers gravely, and was being held in a detention center for deranged animals. Guillaume's name and phone number were on the collar of the dog.

The news stunned Guillaume.

Mustang never hurt anyone before. But then, he remembered the dog's unusual behavior over the last days, particularly those growling and baring of teeth in sleep. Dogs dream what they'll do later—Guillaume knew that for fact, but he had too many other things on his mind then to look after Mustang. He gave up going to the pediatrician and drove to that detention center with Hugo.

From far, they couldn't recognize Mustang behind the bars.

In a week, the dog had lost at least ten kilos. The brilliant luster was gone from his fur, which now looked like a ragged, matted coat.

Then Mustang smelt them and stood up. He raised his snout, cried out the same painful howl, then lowered his head below the shoulders and held their gaze—as if he apologized for all these troubles. The bright light in the dog's eyes was replaced by a deep, mournful sorrow, heightened by the haggard contours of his face, which had thinned from starving and being out in the biting cold.

Mustang advanced with unsure steps as Hugo neared the cage. He sniffed the boy's hand from behind the grill, then went back to the far corner and sat there with his chin on the floor.

Hugo turned and sobbed.

Guillaume saw he was standing exactly where he had first entered the detention hall.

He stepped forward, lifted Hugo off the ground, and buried the boy's face on his chest. But Hugo threshed his legs and beat his fists on Guillaume. The guard lowered his eyes. Hugo writhed and wailed, as Guillaume carried him away from the detention hall. Mustang had to be left there, to be examined by a veterinary expert.

No one could make Hugo eat or drink after that.

They kept a close watch on the boy, but he showed no signs of doing anything stupid. Nor did he show any signs of withering in his will. As if the boy knew something and he was holding onto it.

Three days later, Guillaume received another phone call from that commissariat. The veterinary expert had examined Mustang, and the dog would be put to sleep. Hugo was at his side when Guillaume took the call. The boy refused to open his mouth and close his eyes after that.

Guillaume's former boss pulled his strings and got Mustang's execution delayed by two weeks, so the dog could be evaluated by two more experts, but Guillaume knew that these new experts would not contradict what their first colleague had said. There was little chance for anyone to save Mustang from the needles.

Nevertheless, Guillaume couldn't give up.

It was no longer only the execution of Mustang; the destiny of Hugo lay closely tied to what would happen to their dog.

So far, Guillaume had lost everything. Now he wasn't ready to lose his son too. After all the means to save Mustang ran out, Guillaume left Hugo again in charge of Anaïs, camped on the snow before that detention center, and declared he was going on a hunger strike.

The same evening, Anaïs brought Hugo to his tent— the boy could no longer be contained at home.

The news spread quickly across the region. By next noon, media trucks poured into the town, and animal rights groups rallied all over the streets. The event drew such a huge crowd to the town that the throughway was jammed, and the authorities had to divert the traffic.

The decision to execute, however, didn't alter.

Then Hugo came down with a fever.

By the next evening, his cold turned into bronchitis, and the boy went into delirium. When the ambulance came, Anaïs took shivering Hugo inside the vehicle and pushed Guillaume back—her stern face told him what he already knew. The crowd yelled and raised their fists, as the ambulance carried away the hallucinating boy.

The decision to execute, nevertheless, remained unchanged.

Then a witness came forward. He said he had seen the two injured skiers breaking into a house, when Mustang leaped on them and attacked.

The news surprised Guillaume. Dogs protect only their owner's property, but, given Mustang's state of mind then, he couldn't rule out the possibility of the attack; the dog had an incredible flair for detecting thieves. The animal rights groups marched again, and the mob shouted louder.

The decision to execute, however, didn't budge an inch.

Two more days went. Guillaume's friends and colleagues urged him to end the strike and go back to his son, but Anaïs said no. Hugo's eyes lighted up when he saw his father holding onto the strike. By then, the event had become prime time news on the national television.

Next morning, a veterinarian's car pulled in before the detention center. The doctor came out with his satchel, scanned Guillaume and his tent, then shook his head and went in through the doors. Blood splashed inside Guillaume's chest.

Forty minutes later, the veterinarian came out with his eyes lowered and drove away. Shortly after, Guillaume was called to go into the center. The stunned crowd came out of their stupor and started to follow Guillaume, but he raised his palms and asked them to stay where they were.

The crowd listened to him. The anger on their face changed into fear.

When Guillaume emerged from the center again, with the corpse of Mustang in his arms, Hugo was there at the front of the crowd, staring straight at his face. Anaïs and Louis stood behind the boy.

Guillaume averted his eyes.

He had failed in his promise to his son. He kept his eyes on the ground and walked toward his tent, covering Mustang as much as he could from the glare of media. He didn't stop until he laid Mustang inside the tent, came out, and closed the zipper.

Then he stood up and turned.

His brain squirmed; he still couldn't look at Hugo. He waited for the boy to cry or to run into his arms, but none of that happened. Neither his friends nor his colleagues uttered a word. Only Anaïs came forward and touched him on the arm.

And then, the hell broke out inside Guillaume.

He knelt on the ground, covered his face, and cried.

He cried for long, oblivious to the crowd around him. He didn't care what Hugo or Louis or Anaïs thought about his failure. Then he felt Hugo's hand on his shoulder.

He uncovered his face and stared at Hugo.

The boy's look had changed. From behind those eyes, still framed by the boyish eyelashes, Guillaume saw his own father looking at him—with the same mix of pain and love that said Guillaume had tried, but he could have done better. He wanted to draw Hugo to his chest, but he couldn't. In those last few minutes, the boy had grown up to be a giant, and was now well beyond his reach.

It was Hugo who guided him by the hand to the tent and told him what he must do next.

Guillaume lifted Mustang onto his truck, took down the tent, thanked the crowd for their support, and then started driving out of the town. Anaïs trailed him in her car, with Hugo and Louis. He felt his blood sugar was low, but he knew his mouth wouldn't let any food in now. It was better to get done with what he had to do.

As he passed the town square, he saw the executing veterinarian in his vehicle, sitting with a dark face and smoking nervously. Guillaume's jaws clenched, and his grips tightened on the steering wheel. But then, it wasn't the fault of the veterinarian; the doctor had only executed orders.

The doctor's face became animated when he saw Guillaume coming—as if he wanted to apologize about Mustang—but Guillaume looked straight ahead and drove on. He didn't need lame condolences from anyone, and certainly not from the executioner himself. In the rearview mirror, he saw the doctor fall back into sullenness again.

Past the traffic circle, Guillaume took the ramp and joined the highway.

The midday sun, low in the icy blue sky, blinded him from the front, made it difficult to see in the glare from the snow. He pulled down the visor and kept driving. He was high on adrenaline, and he drove the hundred and seventy kilometers straight, without stopping once. When they exited the off-ramp and entered their village, the sun shone even more brightly above Guillaume's farmstead.

Suddenly, in that abundance of light, his own farm felt like a foreign place to Guillaume.

He couldn't find the exact reason for that feeling, but, more he approached his farm, more distant it seemed to him. And more of everything around that farm became foreign too.

He had lost out big time on that land. Now he didn't want to take his last proof of failure there. Besides, he didn't want to bury Mustang in a place he wasn't sure about any longer.

He crossed his farm and continued driving.

Anaïs honked from behind. Guillaume took out his arm and signaled her to follow. He went past the pasture and the cowshed—in two more months, those wouldn't be his either—then started climbing the trail that wound up through the forest and led to the high pasture where Old Billy was buried.

Anaïs honked again. This time, Guillaume saw what she meant; he stopped.

Anaïs parked her car by the trail. The two boys came out of her car and sat with Guillaume on the front seat of his truck. Anaïs climbed onto the back of the truck and sat with Mustang. Then they took off again for the high pasture.

Guillaume's mobile phone rang, but he couldn't recognize the number. It had to be a journalist. He switched off the phone and shoved it into the glove compartments. He didn't want to answer calls from anyone in these sacred moments.

When they reached the high pasture, he saw he didn't have what he needed for Mustang's burial. The sun was low over the western ridge, but there was still plenty of time to come back and finish the burial. He lowered Mustang's corpse on the snow, then speeded back with the truck toward his farm.

A car was parked before his gate.

The vehicle looked oddly familiar but didn't belong to anyone he knew. It could be one of those media vehicles that flocked before the detention center. The thought irritated him. He wasn't sure, in his depleted state, he could deal with anyone in civility. They were on his property now, violating his rights to privacy. He started thinking about a polite way to make them leave.

The car's door opened.

The executing veterinarian stepped out and walked slowly toward his truck. Blood shot inside Guillaume's head, and he started seeing red flashes. He closed his eyes, prayed to remain calm and not do anything stupid. His temple throbbed, his fingers trembled. The strain and the low blood sugar weren't helping him really.

He killed the engine, stepped out of his truck, and slammed the door. He felt his temper flying; he tried his best to hold it back.

"What can I do for you, Doctor?"

"Have you buried your dog?"

Guillaume ignored the question and kept walking.

He couldn't interpret the look on the doctor's face. If the guy came because of the bites of his conscience for killing a good dog, he should go and talk to a priest, and not to the owner of the dog. He went past the veterinarian and opened the gate.

"Monsieur. Have you already buried the dog?"

"Not yet." Guillaume pulled the gate behind him. "But you're making me late."

"I tried to call you." The man reached into his pocket and pulled out a sheet of paper. "I suppose they didn't give this to you."

"What is it?"

"The death certificate of your dog."

Guillaume held the rein of his temper. "I don't need that." He turned away from the doctor, but his veins kept pulsing.

"Monsieur, listen." The doctor pushed open the gate.

"Get out!" Guillaume couldn't control himself anymore. "If you don't, I'll shoot you."

The doctor stepped back.

"I said, Leave! Right now."

The doctor lumbered to his car but didn't enter the vehicle.

Guillaume took the spade and the shovel from the toolshed, then went past the doctor and threw the tools on the back of his truck.

The doctor still stood beside his car. Guillaume clenched his fists and walked toward him.

The doctor lifted his palms. "I'll go, but please listen."

"Make it quick."

"Can I see the dog?"

"Go see a psychiatrist."

The doctor grimaced. "I hope you didn't leave the dog in the open."

"Enough! The dog is where it should be."

The doctor rubbed his face and entered his car.

An eagle-owl flew out from the hayloft of the barn and cruised over the cowshed toward the pasture. The doctor stared at the buzzard and shook his head. "Monsieur, I hope you didn't leave the dog unattended somewhere."

"Please leave, Doctor. You're making me late for my work."

The veterinarian backed his car up and drove away. Guillaume stood there until the doctor turned on the highway and disappeared in the traffic. The man had killed Mustang, and now he was worried about the dog being left in the open.

What a nut!

Guillaume climbed onto his truck and turned on the ignition. He had wasted time with this crazy doctor, and now the burial needed to be finished before the daylight was gone.

But then, he saw the doctor's point in a flash.

And the flash numbed him thoroughly.

He had left a dead animal out in the open, with two

children and a woman at its guard. He had forgotten about those wolves that prowled the mountains again. His fingers froze on the steering wheel; goose bumps covered his forearms.

How could he be a farmer in the mountain and make such an error?

He jumped out of the truck and darted into his house.

He called the gendarmerie, grabbed his hunting gun, then sprang out of the house and speared off with his truck.

No way could he blame this error on his fast. Over these last months, he had made one mistake after another. Now, if anything dreadful happened to Anaïs and the two kids up there, he would never be able to pardon himself.

As he lumbered up the winding trail, he prayed to God they were still safe.

After his father lowered Mustang onto the snow and drove away to get the shovel and the spade from their farm, Hugo waited until the pickup truck crossed the high pasture and vanished down the trail.

So far, Hugo hadn't touched the dead dog once, not even looked at his corpse closely. He was afraid the floodgate of his tears would be released; he needed to hold that back for uplifting his father. He was stunned when his father knelt before everyone and wept like a child.

Not that he was ashamed of his father or lost any respect for him. But, he was amazed to find out how, inside a man of such great strength, a vulnerable kid of raw sensitivity could exist.

True, Father fought till the end and still couldn't save Mustang. But, in that failure, Hugo saw a side of his father he had never seen before.

That side made Hugo love his father even more. He wanted to protect his father as if he were Hugo's child and not the other way around. There was no way for Hugo to cry before him.

But, now Father was out of his sight, and Hugo could be himself again.

He knelt before the dead dog and rubbed his fur. He felt the eyes of Louis and Anaïs on his back, but this was a time that belonged to him alone. Like Father, Hugo no longer cared what others thought of him. The touch of the fur was fogging his eyes, but he wasn't going to break down. He had things to tell Mustang, and he was going to tell those in the ears of the dog only, in the firm voice he had always talked to him.

He lifted the dog's legs one at a time and slid his hand down to the paw. The limbs were not rigid yet. The rigidity comes many hours after death—he had seen that with those other animals that died on their farm. The dog's muscles had lost their mass, but their fibers still held the power of thunder.

He pulled the dog's lips back and checked his fangs—the instruments that had protected Hugo from intruders of all sizes and shapes. Nothing had changed about those either.

Hugo's throat was beginning to choke.

He lay on top of Mustang and wrapped his arms around the dog's neck. He didn't know where the dog's spirit was right now; but he knew, if he spoke to him sincerely, his words would be heard. He pressed his mouth against the dog's ear and whispered:

"You died, but your love will never die.

"You left this life, but your life still remains with us.

"I know you never hurt anyone without a reason. I'll never believe what others keep saying about you."

Hugo's throat started to give away. His chest was shaking too. He thrust his lips deeper into the dog's ear and yelled:

"I love you more than ever.

"I'll always come back here to tell you my stories."

Hugo's whole body shuddered. He hid his face behind the dog's head and sobbed.

He felt Anaïs's hand on his crown and lifted his face.

The back of Mustang's head was drenched from his tears. His heart still thudded against the dog. For an instant, in between his own heartbeats, Hugo had the impression that another heart beat once or twice. But the illusion passed, and he realized it was his own heart beating at an irregular pace. He combed the fur on the back of Mustang's head, then kissed him on the cheek and rose to his feet.

Mustang's ear, the one Hugo had spoken into, remained folded back and open, as if the dog wanted to hear some more.

But, there wasn't time for any more mourning. Soon Father would return with the spade and the shovel, and Hugo would need to give him strength for the burial. The crying had done him good, though. He felt lighter; his head didn't feel clogged anymore. There were chores to be done before the burial, and crying had prepared him for what he thought he would never be able to face.

Gray clouds, in the form of large cotton candies, hung over the western ridge. Father said, Weather moves from west to east in the north. Those clouds could be here soon, but they didn't look like they would bring down heavy rain. He tried to feel the direction of the wind. Strangely, even at this height, there was no wind at all.

What did that mean?

One never knew in the mountains.

He turned toward Louis. "Help me carry some sticks and stones."

"For what?"

"We need to build a tomb and a cross."

"A cross for a dog?"

Hugo turned and walked away.

"Where're you going?"

Hugo kept walking.

"But everything here is covered with snow!"

Hugo pointed toward the end of the pasture. "If you want, join me in that cave over there."

"And leave the dog with Mom?"

Anaïs yelled: "Louis, go with Hugo!"

"Are you sure?"

Anaïs flung her hand over the head and sat on a rock.

Louis hesitated, and then followed Hugo.

Fresh snow blocked the mouth of the cave. Hugo pushed the powder aside and went in. The quartz rocks were still there, exactly where he had left them before, but the sticks were gone. Never mind. There were logs in the refuge.

One by one, they carried the rocks and placed them beside Mustang.

Father was late, and Hugo couldn't see why. He wondered if Father had fallen sick from hunger and stress, but then he dismissed that fear. No matter how sick Father became, he would never collapse before the burial.

Anaïs was talking to someone on the phone. The person on the other end might very well be Father. Probably, they needed other things for the burial, and he had to go back again. The sun always set later on the high pasture than in the valleys, so he didn't need to worry about anything yet.

Besides, he and Louis still had to collect the logs from the refuge.

He looked at Mustang: the head lay at an odd angle. The neck must have moved when Hugo was lying over him and crying. He raised the dog's head and tried to straighten the neck. But the muscles resisted. And the ear that lay flat before now stood stiff on the dog's head.

The stiffness of death had taken over Mustang finally.

He laid the dog's head on the snow, then left with Louis to collect the logs from the refuge.

The logs were still there at the corner, where Grandfather had left them. Hugo pulled the tarpaulin away and started looking for two stakes that would serve for a cross.

"Hugo, come here!" Louis cried out from the porch. "Quick!"

"What is it?"

Louis swore. Hugo stopped rummaging through the pile and came out on the porch.

"Look." Louis pointed upward.

High above the pasture, three black dots circled. Louis gasped, and his face became white with fear.

Hugo too realized what those black dots were.

And the realization seized his guts.

Everyone knew what happened to animals and people that appeared dead or lay still in the mountains—they all had forgotten about this in the middle of stress. Hugo looked over the trail that came up from the valley, but couldn't see his father's truck anywhere. Anaïs was still talking on the phone.

Hugo knew that these massive vultures had a far sight eight times sharper than men.

He also knew, from where those buzzards were right now, they had very well seen the corpse of Mustang on the snow, and it would only be a matter of minutes before they came down and tore him apart. Even if Anaïs tried, there would be no way for her to defend Mustang alone from their beaks and claws. He and Louis absolutely needed to reach there before the buzzards came down.

Louis was still gaping with fear. This time, it was up to Hugo to take charge of the situation. He grabbed two stakes that looked the sturdiest in the pile, shoved one into Louis's hands, and pulled him out of the porch.

The vultures came quicker than he had thought. The two of them had barely crossed a third of the pasture, when the buzzards were flying over Mustang and Anaïs already, going around in shrinking circles, and descending with every round they took. Two more vultures had appeared higher up in the sky.

They had crossed about half the distance, when Louis stopped and started to sob.

Hugo couldn't believe what he was seeing in Louis. He pulled him by the hand, yelled to Anaïs at the top of his voice, and pointed to the sky. She heard him, looked up, and dropped the phone from her ear. Hugo wanted to sprint, but the loose snow wouldn't let him. They had crossed two thirds of the pasture, when four more vultures appeared over the crest of the mountain and started plunging toward the group that circled below.

Anaïs now stood over Mustang, bending and spreading her arms over his corpse. The buzzards circled barely fifty meters above them, as if trying to figure out the best strategy to break into her defense. Louis vomited. He looked up at the vultures and cursed in rage. Hugo knew the vultures never touched bodies that moved, so nothing would happen to Anaïs as long as she kept moving her limbs.

But, Hugo saw he was wrong about the vultures.

Just when the two of them leaped into the circle under the buzzards, the biggest among them flew up, then swooped down upon Anaïs and hit her on the head with its claws. She stumbled over Mustang and fell on the snow.

Louis shrieked, froze to his feet.

The leading buzzard took off, started to swoop down again, but, before it hit Anaïs, Hugo leaped forward holding his stake in both hands and hit the vulture at its midsection with all his strength.

The log cracked into two. The buzzard gave out a deafening cry and fell to the snow.

But not for long.

The vulture staggered to its feet and spread out its huge wings. Hugo charged at it again with the pointed end of the broken log, but the buzzard hopped off and flew away. All the other vultures took off too and followed their leader's trail.

Anaïs sat on the ground now, holding the other half of Hugo's log with both hands. Louis stood over her and trembled; he could barely hold on to his stake. Blood seeped from Anaïs's head down her cheek. There was still no sign of Father on the trail.

That worried Hugo. Father was never late without a reason. The clouds had combined into a huge mass, and the wind was beginning to pick up now. That wasn't a good sign at all. At least, the sun was still there.

Anaïs was hurt. Louis was not in a state to help. Hugo was going to have to mount the guard. Father did his part when Mustang was alive; now, it was up to Hugo to protect the dog's corpse.

Hugo looked at the tomb of Old Billy. Hadn't he prepared Hugo for this battle?

What would Mustang think if he knew Hugo was

afraid?

What would Father say if Hugo failed?

No way.

If Hugo cowered before this task, he didn't deserve to be a rescuer at the gendarmerie. If those buzzards came back again, he must know what to do. Anaïs and Louis might not know how to lead a battle, but Hugo had sparred enough with Old Billy to have that knowledge.

The best would be, of course, to avoid the battle.

The cave wasn't that far from where they were. The three of them might be able to carry Mustang over there, before those buzzards returned. The flakes started to fall. Which meant the rain wouldn't come most probably. Thank God—it would be easier to carry Mustang through the snow than the freezing rain.

Hugo, at the lead, wrapped his arm around the dog's neck, while Louis and Anaïs held one of the hind legs each. They lifted Mustang off the snow and carried him toward the cave. With the free hand, each carried a log, as a balance to plod through the snow, and as a weapon in case the buzzards came back.

A helicopter crossed the ridge, then hovered over the observatory. Hugo knew they used the helicopter to drop off supplies and pick up garbage. Even if they stopped and waved at the helicopter, the pilot wouldn't see them from this far. It was the best to keep moving with Mustang toward the cave.

Hugo had the impression the dog sighed once.

No, the noise actually came from behind, from either Louis or Anaïs; they were struggling with the weight of the dog. Then he heard the roaring of an engine down the trail. That might be the pickup truck of Father, but, from the way it sounded, the vehicle was still way down from where they were.

Given the conditions of the trail, Father would take at least a quarter of an hour to come up here. And, if it weren't Father coming up the trail, they would have lost time waiting for him. It was better to keep moving toward the cave.

The vultures had given up on them it seemed, but the snowfall was building into a storm. They were barely a hundred meters away from the mouth of the cave. If they kept moving at this pace, they could reach the cave in less than ten minutes, and they would all be safe in there. The helicopter finished its work over the observatory and lifted off.

A gush of wind came from behind.

Anaïs screamed. But, before Hugo had the time to turn, the buzzard hit him on the head. The impact blinded him, made him see the stars. Mustang fell from under his arm. Hugo tumbled over and went face down on the snow.

He scrambled to his feet immediately, searching for his stake.

His head spun, his legs buckled. Louis and Anaïs lay prone, their faces hidden in the snow. A buzzard stood over each of them and pecked at the back of their heads. Hugo grabbed his stake like a spear and charged at the vultures. The two buzzards hopped off and flew away.

Six others had closed in around Mustang. They stood in a circle looking at each other, as if they were afraid to be the first one to reach the dog. The leader of the group was not among them. Hugo raised his stake and leaped into the circle. The vultures flapped away.

Then he saw what it was that made the vultures hesitate.

From the way Mustang had fallen, the skin of his face was pulled to the side, exposing two of his deadliest fangs—as if the dog pulled back his lips in rage and showed his weapons before launching an attack. The hair on the dog's neck stood up too, from being carried by that part under Hugo's arm.

Hugo forgot his pain and couldn't help smiling: even after death, Mustang brought the same terror upon his enemies!

Anaïs screamed again. The leading buzzard hit Hugo at the mid of his back, then crashed down upon him. They thrashed around on the snow, rolling on top of each other, each trying to grab the other by the throat. The buzzard's claws cut through Hugo's clothes and tore away skin from his ribs.

The leading buzzard now stood over Hugo, spreading its wings in victory. The naked neck and the bald head bobbed from its shoulders. And its unblinking red eyes hurled fireballs at Hugo.

Then the monster stepped forward and aimed its beak at Hugo's eyes.

Hugo raised his arms and covered his face.

"Dad! Mustang!"

The beak hit the back of his hand, tore away some flesh.

But then, Hugo thought he heard a low growl. He turned his face under the palms and glanced at his side.

Mustang was rising to his feet!

The dog bared its teeth. The hackles bristled on his back and neck. His sharp gaze fixed on the fiend that stood over Hugo's chest now.

"Get him, Mustang!" Hugo writhed under the buzzard's weight. "Kill—"

The buzzard pecked on his forehead, and Hugo saw the stars again.

Mustang boomed a bark and leaped.

The buzzard fell off Hugo's chest and crashed on the snow. A frenzy of shrieking and barking and zapping and shuffling followed. The powdered snow went flying up and around. Finally, Mustang emerged from that cloud with the head of the vulture in his jaws and speared toward the other two that sat over Louis and Anaïs.

A fire shot in the air.

Through the veil of the flying snow, Hugo saw Father jumping out of the truck and dashing toward them with a rifle. Meanwhile, the buzzard over Louis had lost its head to Mustang.

Father shot in the air again. The buzzard over Anaïs hopped away and took off.

Then Hugo observed something he had never seen before.

Mustang leaped after the escaping vulture. Midair, the dog drew in his limbs together and sprang again! He caught the buzzard by one of its wings and pulled it down on the snow. Next moment, its head was wrenched off too.

Mustang now ran around the snowfield barking at the top of his voice, but the other vultures had flown away long ago. A helicopter had landed on the pasture. From its color, Hugo knew it belonged to the Gendarmerie of the Alps.

Father reached the site of the battle.

The Chief and the paramedic jumped off the helicopter and started running toward them.

Louis and Anaïs were standing now. Their heads and necks bled, but they were smiling proudly at Mustang—who still leaped around the snowfield, barking at vultures that no one else saw.

Hugo's wounds didn't hurt anymore.

The Chief and the paramedic reached them, out of breath.

"Call for backup!" The Chief said.

Anaïs stepped forward. "No."

"Why?"

"The dog is dead."

The Chief's face smoothened. "Right, we didn't see any dog."

Anaïs nudged Father. "Call the vet and apologize."

"Sure." Father's face darkened. "His number is on my phone."

"Ask him for the death certificate too."

"Of course."

The Chief crossed his arms. "Now, what will you do with this dog?"

Father glanced at Anaïs. "We'll move to Jura."

The Listener

The bell rings in three rising tones. We pack our stuff and come out of the class. Down the corridor, the Principal stands in front of his office, with the social worker at his side; both stare at us frigidly. I feel Jerome hesitating beside me.

"See you later," he says.

"Are you sure?"

"It can't be for you, right?"

"You want me to wait outside?"

"Mathew, just go on."

It has to be something about the skate-park again. Odd that I didn't hear anything about it. I look at the other boys who had troubles with that park, but only Jerome enters the Principal's office. Maybe he didn't tell me what else is going on with him. His life isn't easy in that foster children's home.

"Hey, Mathew!" Coralie walks toward me. "You're done with your handcraft project?"

"No."

"What are you making?"

"A barometer. And, you?"

She glances aside. "Not sure."

"When is it due?"

"End of the week."

I shove my hands in the pockets and think. Her face brightens with hope.

"Try a stethoscope," I say.

"What!"

"You need a piece of wood and two metal disks."

"And then?"

"Let's go down."

I take Coralie to the trunk of the tree lying at the end of our courtyard. "Stick your ear to this end." I go to the other end of the trunk and stick my ear there.

I tap on my end. "Can you hear me?"

"Oh, yes!"

"See what I mean?"

She jumps. "You're really a genius!"

"I didn't invent that."

"How did you know then?"

"It's in the books."

We pick up our bags and come out of the schoolyard.

"Want to go to the park with me?" Coralie says.

"I have homework to do."

"Let's go for a hot chocolate then."

"I'm not hungry."

"You're ashamed to play with girls."

"Aren't we beyond that age?"

"Jerome is going to get you in trouble someday."

"Coralie!"

"At least I warned you."

She turns and walks away.

That is the problem: most don't see the true side of Jerome; they only see what they want to see. I doubt if anyone from here ever went inside his foster home—life in there makes mine look a thousand times better. But that didn't stop Jerome from doing what he did for me.

I see a group of kids staring at me and smirking. I know they're talking about me, about my mother and Thierry. I wish my mother waited until the end of my school here before going out with Thierry. Not many parents in this town date the teachers of their kids.

I reach home, but I don't feel at home.

I dump my school bag, ignore the afternoon snack my mother has prepared for me, and sit at my desk. I try to concentrate on what I have to do for my classes, but I can't. Thierry will be here soon. I've had enough of him at the school already. I pack my books and leave for the place I do feel at home.

Thierry is not cruel, though. He doesn't hit me or my mother. I was relieved when she kicked my father out finally. But, she could have waited a few more months before starting her relationship with Thierry—till I finished my primary school here and moved to the middle school at the other end of the town. Well, Thierry might not have waited for her until then. Good friends don't cross my path everyday either.

In any case, I'm leaving Thierry's school this year. Unless I fail the exams. But that depends on me alone.

I cross the paved road and enter the forest. I've forgotten my watch, but there are still a few hours before the sun will sink behind the stone walls of the chateau's park, and the forest will become dark and cold. I have enough time to sit down and revise my lessons. No kids ever go to that part of the forest.

Except for Jerome. But I doubt he'll go there this afternoon. I look back once more, then move on.

On the slope, there is a sign, in green and white. My heart quickens. No, they won't do that here, not this close to our town; people will go crazy with them. I leave the trail and dart up the slope.

I'm wrong. They have tagged the same green sign with a red tape around a tree: 'Danger! Here, the Forest Office is taking care of the trees for you.'

Several times before, I saw this notice at other parts of the forest. Then the danger actually fell upon the trees. Their dead bodies piled up on the eighteen-wheeler trucks and went away. That was fine for me so far, but now they're coming closer to the part of the forest I don't want them to. I turn around and look down the trail.

The trucks have been there today—the dirt is marked with the tracks from their tires. I hope nothing horrible has happened while I was at school. I dash down the trail and stop before the plot.

My tree is still there.

And, the surrounding ones too.

Nothing has changed on this plot. Only the fountain sounds a bit odd from here.

I pee at the side of the trail, on a shiny black centipede; it hurries for cover under the leaves. I smile. The poor insect must have thought hot rain is falling upon it this spring.

My throat feels parched. I drink from the fountain then stroll around. Farther down the trail, the Forest Office has taped out a large area. So that was their sign for, near the entrance of the forest. My ribs loosen. I return to my tree and sit on her root.

The red squirrel drinks from the stream. Then it scurries up the maple tree and jumps onto a branch of mine. That squirrel never climbs directly the trunk of my tree if I sit here, even if Toby is no longer with me. The squirrel now sits on a branch and observes me keenly. It certainly doesn't trust me with the nuts it's hiding in the trunk of my tree.

The squeals come from above, but they're shriller and urgent—they sound almost like a child's whine. I look up. Near the top, shielded by the foliage from the sky, there is a nest! The childish squeals are coming from inside that nest.

Of course: birds have their chicks in the spring.

But I missed that nest before. What's happening to me?

I move to the clearing and whistle. Within seconds, the two adult falcons circle over my tree, then sit near their nest. That chick is so lucky to have parents like them.

I return to the root of my tree and lean against her trunk. The velvety moss makes a comfortable cushion to sit for hours, when I need to be alone and think. Well, not exactly alone. My tree hosts a world of birds and animals and insects, some of which I've been trying to identify for months. They don't bother me, though.

My mother's life would have been so much easier if I could accept Thierry like that into our life, but I can't. His odor bothers me. Since he started sleeping in our apartment, it no longer smells like my home.

Everyone needs a home.

If the Forest Office cut my tree, I wouldn't know where to go. Well, I'm being selfish again. If my tree goes, others will lose their home too.

Can they really cut my tree?

I didn't think so, but now I don't know anymore.

At the center of this plot, my oak tree is the oldest of all. With her trunk more than five meters around, she must be at least two hundred years old. The other trees on this plot are dwarfs compared to her—they may as well be her children.

A tree like mine produces five to six thousand liters of oxygen per year. Or, is it millions? I need to check. They won't take down a tree that makes so much oxygen for us.

But, the problem is: my tree will also make excellent furniture.

The Forest Office already cut a tree like mine at the entrance of the forest. They said it was leaning too dangerously over the water tank. When they need to cut a tree, they always find a reason that shuts people's mouth. My tree is erect and sturdy—she is not dangerous to anyone. But she is too far into the forest; if they took her down, not many people would know probably.

I sit on the patch of grass and take out my books. I still can't concentrate on them.

This plot has been a soothing place for me, since my mother started leaving me at the Children's Center and going away on vacation with Thierry. At first, it felt like a punishment for my behavior toward Thierry. Then I was glad she didn't impose upon me to come with them. I have enough of their bickering at home already. But, what I don't understand is this:

Why does she go on vacation with Thierry always?
Why does she never go with me?

Maybe she loves Thierry more than she loves me.

The thought heats my ears and makes my mouth taste bitter. I search for a chewing gum, but my pockets are empty.

I know I'm hard to deal with. I try to be good, but I can't do any better. I'm glad to spend my vacations at the Children's Center; at least, that way my mother doesn't have to handle my problems during her vacations.

I lie on the grass and rest my head on the books. The soft grass, with its lush smell, soothes me again.

Not for long. I worry about Jerome; I don't like the way he's changing.

This is where I first met Jerome one dawn, when I skipped out of the Children's Center to escape the smelly kids in that tiny room. When I approached my tree, I saw another boy drinking from the fountain. I was scared at first, but that boy didn't claim my tree. He said he had seen me at our school, but I didn't want anything to do with him. He looked too odd for his age.

But, when I fell into the pond that morning, it was Jerome who pulled me out. And then he sneaked out fresh clothes for me from his foster home. If the Children's Center had found all this out, they would have raised a hell with my mother. Since then, Jerome has been my best friend at school.

I try to help Jerome to be better, but I never succeed. The thought depresses me again. I rise from the grass and go around my tree.

My heart skips a beat: someone has driven four climbing nails into her trunk!

It can't be the Forest Office; they use ropes to climb, not a ladder of nails. Some airhead must have taken my tree for Mont Blanc. In fact, I should have been the first to climb her, but I didn't want to bother the animals that live up there. Now I want to see what this idiot has done to my tree. I take off my jacket and reach for the first rung.

The top rung brings me to the place where her trunk forks into three limbs. Hidden among them, there is a pit inside her trunk, filled with dead leaves and twigs and yellow mushrooms, all intact. Whoever came up here didn't go inside this trench. The red squirrel isn't watching me anymore. This must not be the place where it hides its nuts.

I jump into the pit. A greenish brown lizard scampers out, then slithers up one of the limbs. The upper border of the trench reaches my waist. I lean over the edge and look around.

The old plot seems all new from here. This must be the way my tree sees this place too. I should have come up here before. The gurgle of the fountain sounds clearer from here. A sturdy woman goes swaying down the trail. I duck my head and hide behind a limb. She doesn't look like anyone I know from this town.

Suddenly, my tree goes too silent.

I look up. The two falcons sit closer to their nest now. And they have their gaze fixed upon me.

I sigh: they don't trust me with their chick.

Wait. If I had a baby, wouldn't I behave the same way?

Yes.

The leaves don't shield their nest enough from the predators of the sky; and here I am, on this tree, coming up toward their nest. Even if they know me, they don't know what I may have on my mind.

The two falcons are doing exactly what they should do as parents.

I glare at the ladder of nails. Maybe someone wanted to reach their nest and steal their chick. That's why the two falcons are so scared. I'm taking those stupid nails out before I leave.

The head of a brown fox appears from a burrow. It sniffs the air, climbs out step by step, then trots toward the cedar tree. It stops under the branch that almost touches the stream, then turns its head around and looks at me. I wave. The fox lowers its buttocks, pees on the tree, and then enters the underbrush.

I smile.

I'll never claim that tree. I have mine, and I'm happy to share her with the squirrel, the falcons, the lizard, and whoever else lives on her. My tree is big enough for everyone.

I climb out of the pit and go down the first rung to the next. I try to wrench the nail above me with one hand, but I can't move it at all. I try again, with both hands this time. The nail comes out, but I lose my balance and fall to the ground.

I rise. There are bruises on my hip and elbow, but nothing is broken. I've saved another major hassle for my mother. I thank the thick moss, then go to the fountain and splash water over my bruises.

I return with a chunk of quartz and beat the other three nails out of my tree.

They leave holes in her trunk—large enough for my toes, but not for an adult's. Sticky sap oozes out of her wounds. I stand there, scratching my head. Then I know. I fetch wet clay from the fountain and seal her wounds.

That will heal her for sure.

I can't sleep. I hesitate to tell my mother because she has so little time for me these days. Worse, there are no secrets between us anymore. Anything I tell her, Thierry knows—and then everyone else at school. I'm glad Thierry is not living with us all the time yet.

He isn't here tonight. I want to talk to my mother about my tree, but then she'll know I go to the forest alone. Above all, I shouldn't disturb her sleep now. She was tired to her bones at dinner. I know she is being harassed by her boss at work.

I look at Toby's portrait over my bed. It was Toby who dragged me to my tree the first time—maybe he knew what was coming to him. I sit up and start talking to Toby.

"What's happening, Mathew?" My mother stands at the door, arms folded over her chest.

I stammer. She comes and sits next to me. I move away slightly.

She places her hand on my shoulder. "I'll talk to Thierry about getting another dog."

"No, don't." I push her hand away. She doesn't need Thierry's permission for everything. And I don't want another dog anyway.

"What were you murmuring about?"

"Sorry, I woke you."

"Now that I'm up, tell me what's bothering you."

I look at her eyes—they don't lie. I hesitate, then tell her the basics. Her forehead furrows, but she doesn't scold me at all.

"They are cutting some trees so the rest can breathe," she says.

"Those trees need *us* to help them breathe? How did they breathe then, when we were not on this earth?"

"They cut only the sick trees."

"There is a sick tree lying at the entrance of the forest. Why don't they cut that one?"

"Go back to sleep, Mathew."

"I can't."

"Why do you care so much about those trees?"

"I care about *my* tree."

"The Forest Office will never cut your tree."

"You think?"

"They're humans. If you were in their place, would you cut a tree like yours?"

No. I hope my mother is right.

"Can they cut the younger trees on that plot?" I try to imagine my tree without her kids: she looks lonely and miserable.

"No. Go back to sleep now."

She rises from my bed and leaves.

I'm stupid. Those young trees are too small to make wood for furniture. And there aren't too many of them crowding out that plot. So why will the Forest Office cut them? I'm worrying about nothing probably.

But—my mother said absolutely nothing about my going to the forest alone.

What does that mean about her feelings for me?

Our soccer game turns into a fight. The gym guard pulls us

apart then throws us out of the field. I've thrashed the two boys for what they did to Jerome. I try to have a better grip over my anger, but I can't. Now the Principal will call my mother, and Thierry will nod along with her. That's fine. Maybe it will make them see why I wasn't like this before.

The guard has taken Jerome and the two boys to the nurse. I slink across the garden, then climb over the wall and jump into the ditch. A bunch of crows fly up and caw over a bloody pigeon. I chase the crows away and pick up the battered bird.

The poor pigeon's eyes have been picked out; and, the back of its head, smashed. The bird opens its beak a little, painfully. I carry it to the stream, soak the end of my shirt, and drip water into its mouth.

The pigeon swallows a few drops then goes still.

I carry the dying bird to the beech tree and lay it inside a hole in the trunk. The crows or the fox can't reach in there. The pigeon will have a few minutes of peace before leaving this world.

I walk toward my tree but stop: the Forest Office has taped out the plot.

I tear the tape apart and dash among the trees. My head boils, my face prickles. I search for the Forest Office people, but they have left. I fume at the tapes strewn on the ground, but that's not going to help my tree. I sit on her root and try to calm down.

Then I see the differences. The color of the tape is not red but green. And there are no cross marks on the trees.

What does that mean?

"Mathew, what are you doing here?"

I startle and turn. Thierry is walking toward me. I ignore him and go back to what I was thinking.

How did he know I was here?

Honestly, I don't care.

He stops a few meters away from me. "The Forest Office is running a test. You shouldn't be here."

"What kind of test?"

"That's not important for you."

"Will they cut these trees?"

"The whole school is looking for you."

"I'm not apologizing for the punches I threw."

He gapes. "You fought again?"

"Why are they looking for me?"

"Someone tried to lift a kid from the school."

Yeah, right. "So?"

"The point is: you shouldn't be here alone."

"Who told you I was here?"

"I have my eyes."

Wait till I pluck them out one day.

My mother is at home when I return. Thierry didn't lie

about the kidnapper, but he has exaggerated the story to score a point with her. She certainly doesn't want him to spy on me, but he does it anyway—it must be more fun than teaching his boring classes. I can spy on him too, but he isn't worth it really.

What's odd: my mother says nothing about the fight at school.

Has she given up on me?

She only says the red-capped pervert is still at large, and I'm grown enough to know where to put my feet. Then she sits on the couch and looks the other way. That's another change in her these days that I don't understand.

Most probably, I've become less important to her.

I itch around for a while, then go on the internet and try to find out what sort of tests the Forest Office may be running on those trees. There is a good chance Thierry will show up this evening and offer me his bag of advice that nobody wants. I don't want to be in this lounge when he comes in. I know he won't dare coming into my room.

But, he doesn't come tonight. And my mother still looks tense. Maybe they quarreled again over something, as they often do, but that's not my business. We eat in silence. After she tidies up the kitchen, I go near her.

"Can we write a letter to the Mayor?"

She frowns. "About those trees?"

"They're living beings, just like us."

"The Mayor will have a good laugh at that."

"Will you write the letter?"

"Look, Mathew. If you want him to do anything about those trees, you've to show him his interest."

"Like what?"

"Something he can use to win the next election."

That's going to be hard. But then, the idea comes to me.

"How many asthmatics are there in this town?"

"How do I know?" Her eyebrows gather. "But, why?"

"Where can I find that information?"

"Why do you want to waste your time on that?"

I'm going to have to do this by myself. I leave the kitchen and go into the living room.

She comes and sits next to me. "I have something important to tell you."

I tense. Here comes the fight; maybe I'll be suspended from school.

"I'm getting engaged to Thierry."

"What's engaged?"

"We'll marry in the autumn."

I can't believe my ears. "Is he moving in here?"

"No, we're moving out."

"Where?"

"To a bigger flat."

"With me?"

"That depends on you."

Next day, I don't go home after school. I won't be able to do anything there. Even at school I had difficulty hearing what the teachers were saying. I go to the library for a while, then take off for the forest.

The tape around the plot is gone!

The weight lifts off my chest. The Forest Office must have finished their tests and decided to leave these trees alone. I sit on the root of my tree and stretch my limbs. At least this place will remain mine.

I wish I could focus on my studies again.

I don't know where my mother will go with Thierry. Maybe she won't take me with them. I'm not sure I want to go with them either. What choice does a kid of my age have really? I wish I could dive into my studies and forget everything. I could do that only a few years ago, but now I can't anymore.

These days, everything makes me angry.

Except, what my mother announced yesterday. I was afraid I would fly into rage, but that never happened. After the shock passed, I felt calmer; even slept better last night. I don't know what that means.

Maybe it's better for me to go away from my mother. We've gone apart over the last two years, and I think it would be easier for her if I went to a foster home. Maybe Jerome's home will take me in. Life there can't be worse than what I can have with Thierry around us all the time. For sure, I won't hate my mother for sending me to Jerome's foster home.

I lean my back against the trunk of my tree. I wish she could talk. I wish she could help me. I wish she could at least explain to me why things are this way in my life. I don't think anyone can.

But, my tree has her way of caring for me.

When guilt and anger swell inside me, and I can't relax anywhere, she soothes my skin with her bark. She assures me that everything will be alright again. She never tells me how, though. Maybe she doesn't know. Maybe she wants to keep me in suspense.

I believed her at the beginning, but now I'm not so sure anymore.

Smog descends on the plot. The air reeks of rubber, rust, and gasoline. I heard there is a peak of pollution over this region. The authorities have reduced traffic, but the pollution still remains over us.

A masculine woman in high boots strides across the plot, smoking and laughing into her phone. She stares at me for seconds; looks around, worried; then crosses the footbridge over the stream and disappears through the bushes. The smog thickens. It's hard to see even twenty meters ahead. I leave the plot and go toward the pond.

The smog has descended on the pond too. The ducks, barely visible from the shore, remain almost still, quivering only their tails once in a while. On the far shore, the trees stand lumped into a dark green mass, like a ghost waiting for its prey. A waning moon rises over their foliage, but the haze has turned its light into a wedge of blur.

Heavy feet stump toward me. I panic, look for a rock or a stick. But then, Jerome emerges from the fog in his oversized shoes, carrying a plastic bag.

"Hey! I knew you would be here," he says.

"I was going to stop by your place."

He frowns. "Why?"

His tone cools me somewhat. "Will there be a place for me in your home?"

"For you? In my home?"

"Do you think?"

"No."

I don't know what to say. I was hoping he would be jumping with joy. Now I don't understand this boy anymore.

Or, have I become so unbearable that even Jerome doesn't want to live with me?

Probably.

"You came here to look for me?" I say.

"Yeah, but that was for a different reason." He turns to go. "You don't seem to be in the mood for that."

"What do you have in that bag?"

"Bye, bye."

"What is it?"

"You'll see later."

His gestures say it's not something good. Maybe Coralie was right: I should stay away from Jerome.

But then, I don't want to go around with Coralie either. She has her plans to run away from home. I can't say how my mother feels toward me exactly—I'm confused between the way she still cares for me and the way she keeps me out of her life sometimes—but I don't want to run away from home right now.

I wish I knew better how my mother feels toward me.

But, this I know for sure: even if she is seriously disappointed with me, she'll be badly hurt if I flee from this town.

I return to our apartment to finish the letter for Mayor.

I open the botany reference I've checked out from our library.

An oak tree like mine produces about seven million liters of oxygen per year. Let's say, each of the younger trees produces half of that. On that plot, there are my tree plus nine of her kids. Together, they make a total of about forty million liters of oxygen per year. There are some twenty thousand people in our town. So only that plot produces two thousand liters of oxygen per year per person of our town.

That should be enough for the Mayor to win his next election.

My mother becomes serious when she sees the letter. Then she looks at me, her eyes beaming. My chest swells—after all this time, I've made her proud again.

"We should put a price on that," she says.

"Why?"

"Price speaks better than everything else."

Together, we find the price of oxygen and add it to the letter.

"Why did you ask me about the asthmatics?" she says.

"They're the ones who use oxygen, right?"

"No!" She laughs out loud.

I feel stupid, but, at least, I've made her laugh.

"There are people with sleep dyspnea, though."

"What's that?"

"They stop breathing when they sleep."

Uh-huh. "So they need oxygen by their bed."

"Right."

"How many of those people we have in our town?"

"We'll figure that out."

She goes on the site of the Ministry of Health. She finds the percentage of people with sleep dyspnea in France. I multiply that percentage to the population of our town. Then we add that number to our letter too. She seals the letter and hands it to me. I run out and post the letter before the evening mail is picked up.

I'm so happy for the attention she has given me.

Our Mayor replies quicker than we thought: "The letter has been forwarded to the Forest Office."

There it goes. I sit with my chin on the hands.

My mother comes and sits next to me. "We'll go to the Forest Office."

"For what?"

"To save your tree."

She wants to save my tree! I look at her: her eyes tell the truth. Finally she has understood what's truly important to me—and why.

I was wrong about my mother after all.

Now I feel assured. I know when my mother wants something, she always gets it.

But my hope dims as we enter the building of the Forest Office. The man who asks us to wait in the corridor has crew-cut hair, blond stubs over his face, studded rings on his ears, and tattoos all around his arms. The air smells stubborn and cruel around him.

I whisper to my mother: "He takes care of our forest?"

"Yes, he is the Director."

"He looks more like a Nazi than—"

She slaps my arm. "Stop!"

Forget trees. I'll bet this man has no feelings for another human. I stare at the walls of the corridor, count the seconds to leave.

Then the door opens. The Director struts out and waves us toward his office.

"Great letter!" He points his double chin toward the chairs, then stands with his arms crossed over the bulging belly. "Mayor was the wrong person to write, though."

Mother sits, but I keep standing.

"Do you know who owns this forest?" the Director says.

"Us," I say.

"No."

He points to a chart on the walls, with faces connected by lines and arrows. Those faces make me laugh. My mother pulls me onto the chair next to hers.

"Thank you." The Director uncrosses his arms and marches to a file cabinet.

I notice the gun on the wall.

What does he do with it?

He opens the drawer and takes out a folder. He shuffles through the sheets, frowning and swearing, then takes out one. Beads of sweat shine on his forehead. I wonder whether he is angry or nervous with us.

He holds the sheet before my mother. "Look at the figure at the bottom."

"What is it?"

"That's how much debt we have." He glares down upon us. "And the State cut our budget last year."

"How did you get into so much debt?"

"That's none of your business."

"Alright."

"Now stay out of our way."

He smiles, baring his teeth.

My fists clench. I want to bust his paunch and smash his face. But that will cause more problems for my mother. She has already taken the afternoon off from her troubled job to do this for me.

She thanks him for his time, and we come out of their building.

We pull out of the parking lot, but my teeth keep grinding.

"He has his people to feed." My mother glances at me. "That's what he was trying to tell us, in his delicate way."

"What does he need that gun for?"

"To kill animals."

"In the forest?"

"Yes, when there are too many of them."

"There are *never* too many animals in this forest."

"Let's talk about what we came here for." She checks for the traffic signal. "It looks like we can't do much with the Forest Office."

"Can't we call the police?"

"For those trees?"

"Trees are living beings. They can't just kill them like that."

"Police will take us for maniacs."

"Who do you call when someone hurts animals?"

"The Society for Protection of Animals."

"Is there a society for protection of trees?"

"Yes. It's called the Forest Office."

My knuckles twitch. My fingers close into fists again. I look out the window and try to think of something positive.

My mother drops me at the stadium and returns to her work. I watch her leave, then skip athletics and go into the forest.

The wounds have healed on my tree. I clear out the cracked clay with a twig; now the fresh air will dry the wounds faster. A line of ants is crawling up the trunk, but I can't see where they're going.

I take my shoes off and slide my big toe in the first hole. The climb is steep, but so were the walls in my mountaineering classes. After a few falls, I make it to the pit and jump inside.

The ants are going past the pit, along one of the limbs. The midday sun sifts through the leaves and makes it hard to see. I lean outward and squint: they are going toward a big hole about ten meters above. Sticky brown sap drips from that hole, and some wasps are hovering over its mouth and humming.

No, those are bees.

There must be a beehive inside that hole. I've never seen a beehive in the wild before. How much honey does it have? It will be hard to reach there without a rope. Even if I did, those bees would be dangerous—they're already nervous about the ants coming up to them.

I sit on the bed of leaves inside the pit. A tiny hole looks out in front of me. I lean forward. The hole opens up to the fountain, and to the beech tree I took the dying pigeon to.

Did the pigeon die in peace?

I hope. I've had so many things on my mind since then.

I lean back and relax. The brisk air rustles the leaves above; one comes twirling toward me. The falcons squeal, the bees hum. The fountain splashes, the highway drones. My eyes close, as my tree tells me stories.

At dinner, I ask my mother: "Would it help the trees if I prayed?"

"It might."

"Can I pray to Toby?"

"Sure."

I go to my room and kneel under Toby's portrait. I close my eyes and utter a long prayer to Toby. I know he'll do anything for me.

But, he can't do this alone.

Is there a god of dogs?

Certainly. If the god of men looks like a man, the god of dogs has to look like a dog.

I close my eyes again and pray to that god to help Toby.

Then I pray to the god of foxes, to the god of squirrels, to the god of falcons—of pigeons, of ants, of lizards, and of bees. Finally, I pray to the god of trees too. And that god looks like my tree!

Nothing can happen to my tree then. I close the curtains and go to sleep.

I sit up, drenched in cold sweat.

I look at Toby. His tongue still sticks out the same way, but his ears seem to perk a bit more. His hackles bristle too. And his eyes glitter in a way I've never seen before.

"Why did you whimper like that?" My mother stands by the bed.

"Did I?"

She reaches for my cheek—her hand feels like ice. "Go to sleep now. We'll call some environmental groups tomorrow."

"Who are they?"

"They save trees."

"Why didn't we call them before?"

"Can you go back to sleep now?"

She sighs and leaves.

I close my eyes, but sleep doesn't come anymore. Her words assure me somewhat, but something just doesn't feel right.

I'm not sure if it's about the trees.

The Head Teacher announces that our class is going to the sea for a week. That's great! I don't remember much from my vacation by the sea last time—it has been so many years since I last went there with my parents. It will be exciting to go to the sea again, but this time with my classmates.

And I can be away from my mother and Thierry for a whole week. I'm sure they will let me go.

In the courtyard I hear that two more classes are going. Some kids are babbling about what they saw in their last vacation by the sea with their parents. Those few who have never been to the sea are gaping at what they're being told. I also hear a teacher saying that the Mayor has helped the school for the trip, and some rich parents have donated money so the poor kids can go too. No one from these classes will be left out.

That means Jerome and Coralie will come too.

I look for them. I don't see Jerome anywhere, but Coralie stands at a corner, talking to her girlfriends and glancing at me sometimes. I don't know if I want to share a room with Jerome. This will be a good time to make new friends, but the kids are in small groups with those they know already. It isn't easy to make new friends in this town.

"Hey, Mathew."

I turn. Jerome stands at the corner of the building, with the same plastic bag in his hand. His eyes glitter.

"Come here." He lifts the bag. "Quick."

I go near him. "What's happening?"

"Look." He opens the bag.

Firecrackers. "What are you doing with these?"

"Follow me, you'll see."

We stop near the back of our canteen.

"See that corner room up there?" he says.

"The office for the teachers."

"Exactly. Now hold this bag for me."

"What'll you do?"

"Just hold the bag, alright?"

I wish someone would come. Jerome thrusts the bag in my hand and takes out a rocket.

"Don't do this," I say.

"Why?"

"You have so many infractions already."

"You're catching up with me."

"They'll kick you out of this school."

"I want to be kicked out."

"You don't have to be like this."

"Look what I do."

He takes out a matchbox.

"Don't."

"Shut up." He lights a match.

I throw the bag on the ground and grab his wrist.

We scuffle. The lit match falls on the bag. The plastic catches fire immediately.

A total chaos of cracks and booms and hisses follows. Flashes blind my eyes, fumes burn my nostrils. I hide my face and duck for cover, but the rockets are flying in all directions. One spears into our canteen and explodes.

When the frenzy is over, there is no sign of Jerome. But the whole school has come around the building and is now staring at me in disbelief.

The Principal steps up to me. "You did this?"

I hesitate. "Yes."

"Why?"

"I don't know."

Coralie comes forward. "I saw Jerome with a plastic bag."

"That was my bag."

"Where is Jerome?"

"He wasn't here."

The Principal blows. "Did you know firecrackers are prohibited by the law at school?"

"No."

"Do you know what's going to happen to you now?"

"Yes."

"You want to say who made this mess?"

"Me."

"Alright." The Principal shakes his head and turns. "Come with me."

Coralie covers her mouth and sniffles. Thierry glares at me. The fire truck is screaming toward our school already. I ignore the gaping crowd and follow the Principal into his office.

I've been suspended from school for ten days now. The punishment could have been harsher if our canteen caught fire, but my two weeks' suspension is already the longest in the history of our school. At least, that's what Thierry claims. And, of course, my trip with the class to the sea has been cancelled.

Jerome stopped by twice, but my mother didn't let him in. Coralie said, since that incident, he has been behaving better in school. My mother tried to place me at the Children's Center for the two weeks of suspension, but they refused to take me in. She called around for babysitters, found none, and finally took two weeks off from her work. She had to—she couldn't leave me alone at home.

I have no idea what this leave will do to her job. I wish I didn't do this to my mother for helping Jerome.

The worst came, when my mother said: for the two weeks of suspension, I couldn't go out of our apartment. That also meant I couldn't see my tree for that long.

The shock passed. I felt odd in our apartment. Not because I couldn't go to my tree, but because I had lost the habit of being with my mother alone for so many waking hours at once.

She felt uncomfortable too, I suppose. She avoided being in the same room with me and kept herself busy doing all sorts of housework and papers. Then, one evening, she announced she had found a boarding school for me, and I would start there after summer.

To my surprise, I felt relieved.

And I saw her relieved too.

The decision must have been hard for her. But I'm gad she has taken a position about me, finally.

Since then, our relation has become easier too.

We talk again when we eat, we play scrabbles together, and, last weekend, when Coralie came to see me at home, my mother took us both to the swimming pool, and to an ice-cream parlor afterward. I'm too young to know, but maybe this is how it happens: when two people know that their relation is going to end, they come closer.

I wonder if all these activities I'm doing with my mother now will make the sting of pain worse, when time finally comes for us to go apart.

But, for now, I'm happy.

I can concentrate on my studies again.

In fact, for years, I've never studied so well, as I have done in the last few days. I no longer feel afraid of my exams.

Also, my mother and I had the time to find a list of environmental activist groups in the region. We called them together, and they've assured us they'll do everything to stop the massacre in the forest. I don't have to worry about my tree anymore.

What happened at the school is a pity, but, at the end, that curse has become a blessing for us.

A new fear has started in me, though.

Thierry is becoming aggressive. Not toward us, but about his work at school.

I remember that's how it started with my father, when he lost his job for drinking. I'm not afraid of Thierry, but I worry about his not being nice to my mother. I have hard time figuring out where their relation is going.

He doesn't come here that often anymore—maybe it's because I'm at home always—but, at the same time, he and my mother keep looking for a new flat to live together. I don't like the heavy silence that hangs in the car when we go out to see a flat. At first, I thought my mother didn't want to leave me alone at home; but then, I started feeling she brought me along because she didn't want to be alone with Thierry.

I hope Thierry doesn't beat my mother someday. If he does, he'll have the worst of me.

But, how will I know, if I don't live with them?

The thought heats my head. I open the window and breathe outside.

The air stinks of gas from cars. My eyes itch too. Things have changed so quickly over these years since we moved into this town.

I still remember the fresh smell of leaves that the breeze used to bring into my room, when my mother opened the window in the morning. I felt as if we lived in a forest, although we're only fifteen kilometers away from the city. There might have been as many cars passing through our town even then, but their smoke never remained for so long.

Then they started cutting down the trees, first in the forest, and then in different parts of our town. New houses sprung up in their places, almost overnight. The air grew thick, smog hung over our town for days at a time, and the ambulances screamed more often into the senior citizens' building in front of our apartment.

They planted new trees to keep people happy, but most of those trees withered away; some never even took off.

Last year, they took down those huge trees around the skate-park near our school. Then they closed the skate-park too; and, in its place, they built an apartment complex that they call 'ecological'. They never built another skate-park for us. Since then, the kids have been wandering around the town, breaking things and making graffiti over the walls.

The memory makes me bitter. I leave my room and come out in the lounge. My mother is busy doing her accounts on the computer. I open the screen door and go onto the balcony.

The sun is sinking behind the rows of saved trees on the park of the chateau. A flock of swallows fly over our building, diving up and down like butterfly swimmers. They go over the train tracks, and then fly up the road that goes toward the forest. An eighteen-wheeler lumbers down that road, and I don't like what I see on the bed of that truck.

I go to my mother. "Can I go out?"

"No."

"Just for an hour."

"Mathew!"

"Come with me then."

"I have to cook."

I go back to the balcony. The truck is now rolling on the road beside the train tracks. I fetch my binocular and observe the chopped logs on the truck. There is no way for me to tell where those logs are coming from. I'm not sure about the environmental activists anymore.

The door opens in the lounge. Thierry walks into the apartment with his briefcase. I leave the balcony, go into my room, and shut the door.

Thierry comes on his big feet and knocks. "Can you open?"

"I'm busy."

"I have something important to say."

"Keep it to yourself."

"Mathew, listen. I found someone who might help you."

Yeah, right.

"I called the Forest Office."

I startle. "For what?"

"For you."

"Uh-huh."

"I talked to a student of mine. He works for the Forest Office now."

I open the door. "What did he say?"

"Locals have complained against the Director you met."

"So?"

"He'll be transferred out of here."

"When?"

"End of this year."

That's too late for my tree. I close the door again.

The door swings open and bangs the wall.

Thierry heaves in rage. "You're so rude!"

"Stop!" My mother pulls him away by the sleeve. "Don't ever dare."

"I'm going to teach your boy some manners."

"That's my job, not yours."

"Do it then."

"I will. Now go and sit quietly, if you want to enter this place again."

My mother's bed starts creaking. Then come her moans and his groans that I hate the most. I slip out of my room, tiptoe across the lounge, and stop at the front door. Their rhythms quicken, their noises grow louder. I open the latch quietly, step out in the hallway, and pull the door behind me gently.

It's drizzling.

There are cops near the station, frisking a group of rowdies against the wall. I pull the hood over my head, duck behind the parked cars, then take a dark alley toward the park. There is a shortcut there that will take me directly to the forest, without having to pass through the lighted streets.

I climb over the railing and jump into the park.

My stomach goes cold—there are voices coming from nearby. I crawl under the bush and lie there quietly. They're near the water taps. Then I see the tiny red dots moving from one hand to another. I relax. With what they're smoking, they don't have a clue about what's happening around them.

I move through the bush on four, ignoring the creatures that flurry and rattle away from me. Past the baby's playground, there is a hole at the bottom of the fence.

I watch for movements on the street, then crawl out from under the railing.

The windows looking over the park have their shutters closed. The paving stones glow under the streetlights like in ghost movies. I climb the stairs and reach the road that leads to the forest. Two cars come from my left. I hide behind the lamp-post and wait for them to go by. Then I dash across the road and stop at the edge of the forest.

Two glowing eyes watch me from a bush.

There are no dangerous animals in this forest. From the height of those eyes above the ground, I figure it's one of those foxes that roam through our town at night. The moon hides behind the clouds, but the drizzle and the lights over the city have given a milky hue to the sky. A striped owl flies overhead, sits on a branch, then turns its head and nods at me. I ignore the burning eyes in the bush, climb the slope, and enter the forest.

A black cat bounces out of the bush and hurries toward a house by the road.

Mist veils the trees. The air smells of wood and gasoline. Slick rivulets slide down the muddy slope and gather into the tracks left by the trucks. A chopped log has fallen from those trucks. It lies on the side of the trail like an arm cut off from a body.

The tweets and the rasps and the creaks stop as I go past the trees, glancing over my shoulder every other step. Then I stop looking behind. The kidnapper won't be in the forest at this hour preying upon children. I squint through the shadows, go along the wall that separates the forest from our school, and arrive at the plot where my tree is.

My tree stands out bizarrely.

I have never been here at midnight. Is it the mist and

the milky sky that make her appear like this? I rub my eyes and look again. As my eyes focus, my limbs begin to freeze.

They have cleared out all other trees from the plot.

And my tree stands like a mother who has lost all her children to the war but still refuses to give away her dignity.

The cut trees are not even on the plot. The Forest Office has chopped them into pieces and stacked them into a pile several meters high by the trail. Soon the truck with the crane will come and carry them away. For some strange reason, they've left my tree intact.

Why did they spare my tree?

My prayer has worked.

I look at my tree again, standing alone. The empty plot makes her look bigger and calmer.

There is comfort in her size and quietness. Now I understand why she has become my shelter. I need her tranquil force to feel secure in life. I no longer feel afraid of the dark, nor of the kidnapper. Step by step, I walk into the plot and sit on the root of my tree. I don't know what I would do if they took her down.

The rain has stopped. The plot feels desolate and eerie. Even the stream runs with a sound of sorrow. I close my eyes and lean back on her trunk: she mourns in poise. How awful she must feel to see her children battered and chopped! From the size of their trunks I can tell they've been with their mother for at least twenty years. That's almost double the time I've been with my mother.

But, I'm the one responsible for this tragedy. If I didn't put my stupid nose into the matters of the Forest Office, these trees here would have lived probably, at least for a few more months. Maybe, by that time, the Director would have been transferred somewhere. I'm sure he has done this as vengeance for the challenge we gave him in his office.

Anger starts to swell inside me, but it's not going to help anyone.

Worse—my anger can hurt my tree even more.

I rise from my seat, then drag my heels around the plot and touch the stumps on the ground. Fresh saps still ooze from them and fill the air with the smell of beer.

The mist has cleared somewhat, and a few stars try to twinkle on the dome of the sky above the plot. Under them, the stumps in the ground look like kids who have been buried up to their necks and their heads sawed off in ragged strokes. My throat thickens. I wander away to the far end of the stream and sit on a stone.

I mourn in silence. The mourning calms me somewhat. I return to my tree and sit on her root.

Vapor rises from the stream and disperses into the shrubs around. I look up. A dark cloud still hides the moon completely. The sky, however, is now buzzing with stars—all full of life. Suddenly, I want to leave this world and become a star among them.

My mother will feel sad for a while, but then she'll continue her life with Thierry, without any more troubles from me. Coralie will miss me too, but only for a few days. Then this world will go on as usual, without me. It's better for everyone that way, probably.

The thoughts don't make me sad but open my chest. I stand up and walk around the plot.

I stiffen.

There is a trace of cigarette smoke in the air.

It's coming from the direction of the footbridge over the stream.

I fall on four and crawl to my tree. I squint, see nothing, but hear swishes and crunches from the bush behind the bridge. My skin tingles. I scramble up my tree, holding my breath and praying not to fall. I reach the pit where her limbs fork and slide inside her trunk.

The silhouette of a man has appeared on the bridge.

I hope he hasn't seen me already. My heart thuds, my lungs wheeze. I kneel inside the pit and peep through the hole.

Now the man stands at the edge of the stream, looking up and down my tree. There is a cap over his head, but I can't see its color. I move away from the hole and close my eyes.

Did he see me?

No. He won't be standing there then.

Even if he saw me, what could he do?

Not much. There is no way for him to come up here; the holes are too small for his feet.

I feel better. I look out the hole again.

The man paces along the stream, his head lowered in thoughts, and his hands clasped under the rucksack on his back. He stops, takes out what looks like a cigarette, and fires a lighter. The flame glows the side of his face, his beard and moustache. Then I see the color of his cap.

It's red!

My limbs go numb. The kidnapper has been hiding so close to our school, and the police have no clue about it.

He finishes the cigarette and swings the rucksack off his back.

He takes off his shoes, and then his clothes one by one, with his back turned toward me. His torso is bursting with muscles. His limbs are thick and round. His waist and the buttocks seem a bit odd; and there is a bow-shaped space where the two thighs join. He removes his cap, rubs his face from one side to the other, then steps into the stream.

He stays in the shadow, under the branches of the cedar.

My eyes have become used to the dark now, but I still can't see what he's doing down there so quietly. I wish the moon were not veiled by the clouds. I want to see his rucksack and clothes better, so I can tell the police.

Then the man splashes through the water and rises from the stream, now with his front toward me.

It's a woman!

She hugs her arms below the breasts and goes to the rucksack on the tips of her toes.

She digs into her bag, pulls out new clothes and shoes, then stands up straight. The beard and the moustache are gone from her face. She steps into a skirt, pulls a sweater over her head, then tilts her head to the side and wrings the water from her hair.

A sneeze escapes me before I can put my hand over the mouth.

She startles.

She looks around her, stiff and puzzled. For a second, she looks in the direction of my tree. Then she folds her old clothes neatly, puts them into the bag, and wears her shoes. She lights another cigarette, swings the rucksack over her back, and starts coming toward my tree. I move away from the hole and hold my breath.

She scratches her soles at the base of my tree and coughs. The smoke from her cigarette seeps into the pit. I cover my nose and mouth, pray not to sneeze again.

The bees hum suddenly, and the two falcons squeal

above—the smoke must have reached all the way up to them. She grunts and snorts. She kicks my tree a few times. Then she squishes away, coughing and swearing.

I breathe again and look out the hole.

She sways her hips over the footbridge and disappears into the bush. My throat feels parched, and my tongue sticks in the mouth. I wait for my quaking to stop, then climb down and sprint all the way to our apartment.

The soft breathing of my mother assures me again. I stand still in the corridor for a while, then tiptoe into my room. My legs feel like cotton, and my body weighs a ton. I gulp the water by the bed, then pull the blanket over my head and shut my eyes.

But, the blanket doesn't hide me enough.

I turn under the cover, searching for a position of comfort, but find none. I try hard to forget what I've just seen. But, harder I try, clearer the images come back to me. I try to think thoughts of courage, but the only thought that comes to me is: what could happen if that red-capped woman got hold of me?

I push the cover away and stare at Toby. He says it was stupid of me to go there without him.

I shudder from head to toe. I want to run to my mother. I want to slide into her bed and hold her tightly. But, she isn't mine anymore.

That isn't her fault entirely. I haven't made her feel like my mother for ages.

I reach for the stuffed elephant, one that I haven't touched in years. I draw it close to my chest and whisper my fear in its ears.

The elephant whispers its love back to me.

I wrap its trunk around my mouth and stifle the sob coming.

The police pick up Jerome from school before lunch.

We wait in the corridor to figure out why. Over the week and a half that I've been back to school, Jerome seemed quiet and normal to me. Even though I don't hang around with him anymore, I didn't see anything dangerous about him. I thought the incident around the firecrackers had changed him finally.

Then the rumors come along the corridor.

Apparently, someone saw Jerome hurling a stone at the ecological apartment complex that stands over our skate-park now. The stone crushed a window pane, smashed someone's face, and sent the person to the emergency room. If all that proves to be true, we won't see Jerome in our school for a long time.

Maybe never. I leave the corridor and go down the stairs.

What's odd: when the police took Jerome away, he looked completely poised.

Maybe he's happy to leave us. Maybe he is happy to go from this town. Maybe this happens to all kids in a foster home. More I try to forget Jerome, more his thoughts come back to me.

I still believe that the boy is good inside. He has wits and courage that few in our school have. Maybe that is his problem. He is too different from the rest of us; that's why others don't understand him and treat him like a weirdo.

He wasn't like this when I first met him. Little by little, he became what others wanted him to be.

What a pity!

I wish I could have helped him in some way. But it's too late now.

I don't feel like being in this school anymore. I go to the canteen with Coralie, but I can barely stand the food. After a while, I tell her I want to go.

I sneak out of the school and head toward the forest.

The storm last night has uprooted a massive tree, which now lies across the trail.

The soaked leaves, still dripping, try hard to smile, but then give up. The dogs I know walk on stiff legs today, with shoulders drooping and eyes gloomy. I ignore the questioning looks of their owners and trudge down the trail. Even the birds look down at me with gloom in their eyes.

I hear cawing and squealing from farther down the trail. I think I hear a saw too. I want to reach there faster, but my legs hold me back. I turn the bend in one breath and see the red tape around my tree.

I can't believe what my eyes are seeing.

They've already cut the top branches of my tree. Up there, a man hangs from a cord and saws one more of her limbs. The two falcons fly in panic over what's left of her foliage, squealing and dispersing the crows that caw above their nest. Another man drives a forklift that carries her chopped limbs toward the pile, which has risen by several more meters.

My heart throbs, my muscles pump. I dash into the plot and jump over the tape.

The sawing overhead stops. The man up there yells. His colleague driving the forklift stops, turns toward me, and grimaces. I throw my schoolbag and take off my jacket. It's going to be either me or them.

The man leaves the forklift and swaggers up, chewing. "Little chimp, what do you think you're doing?"

"Stop hurting my tree."

"Your tree!" He grins at the man hanging above. "This punk here says his parents bought him this tree."

"Kick his ass and throw him out."

"Did you hear?"

I pick up a rock. "Try and see."

His chewing stops, his grin vanishes. He takes a step back and frowns.

What a coward!

His hanging colleague climbs down and glares at me. "These are *our* trees, you understand? We can do anything with them."

"Not this one."

He points the saw. "You want me to chop you off with that tree?"

"Do it, if you have the guts."

He steps forward.

I raise the rock and cock my arm. "One more step, and you lose your eyes."

He springs back, holding my gaze. Then he bares his rotten teeth and shakes his head at the other man. They walk away from my tree, huddle at a corner, and then call someone. I lower my arm, but keep the stone in my hand.

The cawing overhead has stopped. The two falcons sit near their nest and watch me, with admiration in their eyes. My back straightens. I strain to hear their chick, but it must be too scared to squeal. The sun is trying hard to shine on the foliage, but the rolling clouds are blocking its path. The red squirrel sits on the maple tree and watches me intensely.

Don't worry; you can trust me this time.

A jeep rumbles down the trail and screeches to halt. The fat Director rolls out and thumps toward me.

"Don't we know each other?" His eyes stay on the rock in my hand.

"Yes."

"Where is your mother?"

"At work."

"You should be at school."

"I am where I should be."

"Do you want me to call your school?"

"Go ahead, but don't touch my tree."

He steps closer. "I'll drag you out by the ear."

I raise the rock. "If you touch me, I'll smash your face. Then I'll have my mother denounce you to the police for touching me."

He shrinks back immediately and narrows his eyes.

They are all coward alike.

"You know police can take you in for skipping school?"

Yeah, right. "They have more serious things to take care of."

He screws his face. Then he sways away, snorting. The two other men squat near the pile of logs and watch the Director with amusement. He swaggers up to them, grunts a

124

command, but the two men shake their heads and look away. The Director points a finger at them and yells, but the two men pay no attention to his words.

The poor Director throws up his hands and takes out his mobile.

He sticks the phone to his ear, sits on a log, and leans against the pile. He scratches his hanging chin for a while, then starts barking into the phone. Whoever he's yelling at doesn't seem to agree with him.

I have just saved my tree!

The rain starts. The wind picks up and sends the clouds toward east. The sun smiles once or twice in between them. Then a gust sways the foliage above and slaps a sheet of rainwater across my face. I look at my schoolbag on the ground. My mother will scream when she sees the books inside. I know her money is tight, but anyone in my place would have acted the same way this morning.

The Principal comes running into the plot, and Thierry trails him. They stop before me and stare at the rock in my hand.

"What are you doing here?" the Principal says.

"Defending my tree."

Thierry grabs me by the arm. I wrench my arm off and raise the rock.

"Don't touch me! Unless you want trouble."

"How long are you going to stay like that?"

"As long as needed."

"They'll cut the tree at night."

"I'll still be here."

The Principal frowns. Thierry takes out his phone and calls my mother. I don't care what she says. If they cut my tree, it's going to be over my dead body. Thierry closes his phone and tells the Principal that my mother is on her way. We stand there, trying to stare each other down.

My mother comes huffing down the trail.

"Mathew! What the hell are you doing here?"

"What does it look like I'm doing?"

"Can I not even work in peace?"

"I'm doing my work here too."

"No, you're not!"

"Just go, alright?"

"Excuse me?"

"I said: leave me alone."

Mother lunges forward. I hurl the stone; it hits her on the face, and then bounces off. She gasps and falls back, holding her cheek. I scream and cover my eyes.

A storm of slaps hits me, throws me to the ground. Thierry stands over me—his eyes glowing red, and his hand still raised. I rise to my feet, searching for another rock around; my ears keep ringing.

"Thierry!" My mother stands up too. "If you hit him once more—"

Thierry's backhand smashes my face, sends me reeling to the root of my tree. I reach out for another rock, but my head spins and my eyes blur.

Thierry raises his hand again. My mother jumps. She shoves him to the ground then bends over him. "Loser! It's over between us."

Thierry heaves on the ground, looking from her to the Principal.

The Principal turns his face away and looks at his feet.

Thierry rises slowly, eyeing my mother from the corner of his eyes. I know those motions, I spring to my feet. He turns abruptly and swings his fist at my mother. I leap, catch his hand midair, and sink my teeth on his forearm.

He yelps like a wounded dog until I let go his arm.

He takes a swing at me. I duck. The Principal catches him by the collar and pins him against my tree. The Director and his two men surround us now. Their eyes glitter; they're excited about what they hope will follow.

But, Thierry doesn't fight back the Principal.

And, the Principal lets go off his collar. "We talk in my office tomorrow."

Thierry ignores the remark and walks out of the plot, wiping blood from his arm.

The Principal offers a tissue to my mother. "Do you want me to take you home?

"No." She looks at me; her cheek is beginning to swell. "Not unless Mathew comes along."

"I'm not coming."

"Mathew." The Principal squats before me. "Your mother needs to take care of her face."

"Let him stay here." She sighs. "He needs to grow up and face the reality."

"That's good!" The Director turns toward his men. "Now, you two get back to work and show this kid the reality."

"No!" I block their path and spread my arms across my tree.

The Director plants his feet before me and crosses his arms over the chest. "You've wasted a lot of our time. Now, get out of our way!"

I aim my head at his belly and charge like a bull.

But, before I hit him, two hands grab me by the arms and jerk me backward. I curse the Director, spit at him, as my mother and the Principal pull me away from them.

They hold me by the fountain while the two men set out to work.

The Director lights a cigar, leans back against the pile of logs, and watches the progress of the slaughter. The massive pile makes him look like an evil, fat dwarf. I've never hated someone like this before.

The branches fall one after another, but my tree stands upright without a quiver. I want to be like her, but my limbs keep shaking. My mother's hand is trembling too.

The saw falls from above. Screaming and squealing and scrambling come from the top. The man up there covers his face. The two falcons scuffle around, picking him with their beaks and claws, and hitting him with their wings. The Director yells, asks him to come down and get the saw. Then he leaves the pile of logs and struts toward his jeep.

He returns with the gun I saw in his office.

My arms swell, but the grips around them tighten too. The hanging man has come down and picked up the saw already. But, the Director orders him to wait and walks toward the center of the plot. The two falcons have returned to their nest.

The Director fires a shot that sends the two falcons flying. The red squirrel falls from its place, but then grabs a branch at the last moment and scurries back up. Black clouds swirl across the sky and block the sun. Wet air brings the smell of firecrackers—that must be the odor of the bullet from that gun. The two falcons return and strive to hover over their nest against the strong wind.

Another shot fires. One falcon crashes to the ground. The other screams in despair, swoops and sweeps over the foliage, then spears into the sky. A third shot goes off and brings that falcon down.

The Director stands the gun against the pile of logs and barks at the man with the saw. The man climbs my tree again and starts sawing.

The branch with the falcon's nest cracks and comes crashing to the ground. The nest ejects from its place and hurls the chick out. The squealing chick rolls over and over, then struggles to its feet, spreads its wings, and opens its beak.

I want to run and pick up that chick. I want to grab that gun and kill the Director. But, my mother and the Principal are bearing down on me.

The gun fires again. The chick tears into pieces.

My mother gasps; the Principal swears. The torn head of the chick opens its beak one more time, and then closes slowly.

My mother releases my arm, covers her mouth, and starts sobbing. The Principal too lets my arm go.

Now I'm free. I can grab that gun with the speed of light, then bust the belly of that monster and smash his head. But my legs have rooted firmly into the ground. And my tongue has lost its power too. A strange calm is taking over me, slowly.

The man up there screams in panic. The saw falls to the ground again.

A thick cloud of bees swarm around his hanging body and swallow his muffled screams in their drones. My tongue prickles; blood pumps inside me again. I want to clap, I want to jump and applaud the bees. The hanging man keeps jerking his limbs, then covers his throat and goes quiet.

They pull the stung man down and lay him on the ground. I hope he is dead.

But, he is not. He raises his head—his face red and blue. He bares his teeth and swears at the bees, but they have returned to their hive inside my tree. The Director hands him the saw and whispers something in his ear.

The stung man springs up and marches with vengeance to my tree. He turns on the saw and cuts a groove around her trunk. My heart shrieks. I close my eyes and pray to Toby. An odd warmth starts to spread across my body.

The saw hauls and roars. I keep my eyes closed and go on praying.

Then I feel Toby's breath on my neck.

I turn my head and look over the shoulder—it's my mother, sighing and wiping her face. The swollen cheek covers her left eye now. A pain stabs me in the ribs, but this is not the time to repent for what I've done to her. I turn toward my tree and go on praying to Toby.

The two men are using a much bigger saw now. The vibration shakes the upper limbs of my tree, but she holds her trunk completely still. I stop moving too. I hold my head upright like her. They've tied three ropes around her massive trunk and attached them to the ground on the left. The Director has returned to the pile of logs and is now smoking his cigar again, with a smirk on his face.

For some strange reason, his smugness doesn't bother me anymore.

My mother wraps her arm around me. I push her hand away; I don't want to soften at this moment.

Now I know my tree will go down.

But, I want to see her going down in pride. I hate to give in like this, but there is nothing more I can do about it. The same odd warmth fills my chest. I feel a sort of poise I've never known before. This must be the last lesson my tree is giving me before she goes.

Her trunk starts to lean away from the ropes.

The ropes snap. A deafening crack erupts from the base of her trunk. The two men cry and dive out of her way. She hits the ground with an explosive thud.

The earth quakes, logs go flying. My tree topples and tumbles. Then she rolls into the stream, splashing water all over the place, and comes to rest.

An eerie calm settles over the plot.

Suddenly, a hustle starts in the pile of logs by the trail.

The two men yell. The Director looks over his

shoulder. The logs come roaring down and bury him without a trace.

 The two men dash to his tomb, strive to push the logs away.

 But, the logs are too heavy to move.

We pull out of the parking lot of the children's hospital. After ten days in that tiny room, I'm glad to be out in the fresh air again. My mother drives in silence, and that suits me perfectly. I don't want to talk about those things anymore. We leave the main road and drive up the street that leads to our home.

 We pass before the shops and the station. This town feels so different now; I don't know if I can live in this place again. At the traffic circle, my mother turns not toward our building but toward the street that I take everyday to school. I don't want to go that way.

 "Where are we going?"

 "You'll see."

 The midterm vacation started while I was away. The town is empty of kids; they have either left with their parents or gone to their grandparents. I don't have grandparents who will take me in their home. The Children's Center won't accept me either. I don't know where I'll go until our school starts again. I don't think my mother can take any more time off from work.

I can't go to the forest either. I still can't imagine that place without my tree. The sting numbed somewhat while I was in the hospital, but, now that I'm back in this town, the pain is returning with a new vengeance.

We go past the Children's Center. Then my mother takes the narrow street that climbs toward our school. I wonder what happened to Jerome. I wonder what my classmates said about me. I wonder what Coralie is doing right now. Nobody was allowed to visit me in the hospital because of my meningitis. I didn't think about them either, while I was away. But, now that I'm back here, I want to see them again.

What does that mean about my feelings for this place?

We pass before the boring ecological apartments that stand over our skate-park; then before the closed gate of our school, where the quiet yard waits sadly behind the railings for the kids. We pass the wall of our school, then my mother pulls into the parking lot before the forest and stops the engine. That's exactly where I don't want to be.

"What are we doing here?"

"Mathew." She touches my forearm. "Will you give me one more chance?"

I know she has broken up with Thierry, but that's her business. I just don't want to be near this forest without my tree. I don't want to be in this town anymore. I want to go away to the boarding school right now.

She opens the glove compartment and takes out a letter with the stamp of our Town Hall on it. I hope she got the financial aid from them to send me to the boarding school.

"There are a few things I want to talk to you about," she says.

"Can't we talk at home?"

"No."

She takes her purse and steps out of the car, with the letter in her hand.

Why did she have to bring me here to show that letter?

I don't know any longer. I open the door and step out.

The chilly air makes me shiver. And it suffocates me more than the hospital. My mother locks the car and starts up the slope toward the trail. Let her go where she wants. I stand with my hands in the pockets and stare at the empty space where the kids gather on schooldays.

She stops and looks back. Her eyes glisten; they implore me without a word. I fidget, and then inch up the slope, looking for something familiar to hold on to.

I find nothing. The dogs I know have left for vacation with their owners. The birds have fallen silent too. Even the smell of this forest has changed.

Suddenly, I know where my mother is going. I try to stop, but my feet keep moving. She doesn't glance back at me anymore. I look over my shoulder, at the desolate part of the trail we've already covered. I want to run out of here, but my legs don't obey my will.

We bend around the boundary of our school and reach the place I fear the most.

Now the whole plot stands completely bare. They've removed my tree from the stream and the logs that were strewn around the trail. The patch of grass has been destroyed too. The red squirrel has already made the maple tree its home. My mother crosses the plot and sits on the stump of my tree. I stop. I can't believe she is doing this to me.

I wait for her to look at me but she doesn't. She opens the letter from our Town Hall and starts reading it. I pray to Toby she has received the money for my boarding school. Nothing else will make me happier right now.

I inch across the battered grass and stand before her.

She looks up. "The Mayor has written to you."

To me! "Why?"

"A new Director has been appointed for this forest."

"I don't care about this forest anymore."

"Yes, you do. And I'll make you see why."

"Why has he written to *me* about that?"

"He knows you wanted to save this forest."

He is wrong. I wanted to save only my tree and her children. And, I haven't.

"What has he written?"

"The new Director has promised not to cut so many trees. And he'll plant new trees on this plot."

In the place of my tree? Blood shoots into my head.

"I don't want another tree here!"

My head spins. I feel like I'm going to faint again.

How can adults be so cruel?

It's already hard enough to see the stump of my tree in the ground. I don't want them to haul that out too, and put another tree in her place. Her stump would at least give me a place to sit, if I ever came back to this town.

"I know how you feel about your tree, Mathew." My mother coughs. "I know how you feel about everything else that has happened in our life recently." She stands up. "I'm still your mother. All I'm asking is: just give me one more chance."

"You didn't have to bring me here for that."

"Yes, I had to. You need to see something about your tree, which I'm sure you haven't seen yet."

"There is nothing more to see."

"Yes, there is." She holds my gaze. "What seems like a defeat to you is actually a victory. That is, if you look at it from a new angle."

"What angle?"

"You did all you could, to save your tree."

"I've failed."

"But your tree has become a hero."

"Pardon?"

"It has sacrificed its life to save this forest."

I startle.

Her words echo inside my head then sink in my chest slowly. My ribs loosen. But, a spasm starts crawling up my throat. I squeeze my lips and swallow the saliva.

"Your tree has made me see my errors too." Her voice has become hoarse. "I saw how I was losing you to this world."

Pressure builds inside my head. I don't like what her words are doing to me.

She steps forward. "Look, what I've bought."

I glance at her hand. She is holding two train tickets.

"Remember that old monastery? Remember that breakwater over the sea?" She cants her head. "Remember how you used to push your stroller over that wall?"

No, I don't.

"Remember that puppy you found on the beach? Remember how you held onto it, when the owner came to take it back from you?"

Of course, I do.

Now the memories flood back to me. My throat throbs, my lips tremble. I don't want to remember those days from the past; they only make my present unbearable. I clench my teeth and hold my breath, but my eyes are betraying me already.

"That's where I'm taking you tomorrow, for two weeks."

I avert my eyes. Two drops roll off my cheeks before I can do anything about them. But, the tears clear my head.

I don't want to fall in that trap. I don't want to be deceived again. I want to go away from all this, for ever. And I want to tell her that, without hurting her feelings, but I don't know how to do that. I stand quietly, twitching my toes inside the shoes. I hope she doesn't take my silence for 'yes'.

She blows her nose. "Before we go there, I want you to do something. Look at me."

I can't. I'm afraid I'll lose control and give in to her.

She lifts my chin. "Mathew."

I open my eyes and look at her.

The mascara has smeared her eyes and is now flowing over the bruise on her cheek. But her pupils have dilated the way they used to before, when I was a toddler. I can't handle what her eyes are doing to me.

She holds my face in her palms. "You have a good heart, Mathew."

I squeeze my lips tighter.

"Now, stop fighting everything."

I wish I could.

"The whole world is *not* against you."

I want to believe that, but I can't.

She draws me closer and wraps her arms around me. "Drop your defense."

I have no idea what she means, but her smell feels good.

"I know it's hard." She rests her chin on my head and rubs my back. "Do you want me to tell you how you can be yourself again?"

My body feels slack. My head is empty. I hide my face in her chest and nod.

"Start by calling me 'Mom'."

I stop breathing. I hear the thudding in her chest.

"Try, Mathew."

I pull her head down and whisper the word in her ear.

The Sacrifice

The fox howled, but louder this time. And closer. François sat up, rubbing his eyes. No heat wave came over him this time, nor did any fatigue. In spite of his anxieties, he had slept well through the night. His mind felt clear. He could get a better grip on the situation now.

Arthur murmured in the next room.

François went over, leaned against the door. He had forgotten to close the curtains last night. The kid's chest rose and fell under the bright moonlight, and a twisted smile lingered around his lips. The church had fed them well last evening. But, it was still amazing how Arthur always slept like an angel, after all that he had lived with Marlene. Maybe all children slept like that when they felt they were out of danger.

François wouldn't know; he never took care of Marlene when she was growing up.

He wasn't even aware of Marlene's existence until she was nineteen, when she came over to France and claimed her right to be his daughter. She was already beyond all help by then. François closed the curtains and stepped out of Arthur's room.

The fox howled again.

The howling didn't come from the woods behind the

building; it came from somewhere near the front.

François went into the living room and stood at the window. The trees across the street quivered in the breeze, cast oblique shadows over the short, thick bushes along the train tracks. The howling probably came from those bushes. Since they thinned out the neighboring forests, the foxes had been wandering around the town at night, scrounging through the garbage bins along the streets for food.

Then he saw the fox.

It was not hiding in the bushes; it sat right on the front stairs of his building and looked up straight at him. He had never seen a fox so close. He opened the window and bent over the railing. The animal rose but didn't panic. It stood in poise, holding his gaze. Probably it understood what was going on in his mind. Then it turned slowly and went out through the gate.

François stood at the window, feeling relieved but empty. He didn't believe in omens; he wasn't going to let those affect him now. He had taken charge of difficult situations before, and he could do it again.

The only difference was: with Arthur around, he couldn't afford to fail now.

Yet, Arthur's presence also illuminated his life.

The eastern sky turned violet then orange. Two large clouds sailed from northwest and covered that spectacular array of light. That's fine. Doubts came, but they always left when he went into action. He had to set the priorities for the day, and dawn was the best time for that. He stepped back and closed the window.

He went into the bathroom, splashed cold water over his face and neck. The chill wiped out his anxiety, boosted his spirit.

He opened the bag of clothes they had collected from the church last night. The winter jacket was a bit large for Arthur, but the boy wouldn't need it for another two months. François filled the basin with soap and water, then started washing the clothes one by one.

When he came out of the bathroom, the rest of his inertia had vanished, and the sun had lit the footbridge over the railway tracks. The day laborers filed over the bridge, waiting for the construction trucks that would hire them for the day.

François went into the kitchen and left the water boil in the kettle.

A fourth of the baguette was still left from yesterday, which could serve for Arthur's breakfast; and the leftover from the church, for his dinner. The lunch he always had at his school, so no worries. An adult can skip meals, but not a twelve year old child. By the end of tomorrow, the monthly unemployment allowance would come in. François poured the boiling water over his tea bag.

The tea tasted bitter than usual.

All these struggles wouldn't be there if his publisher had paid his royalties on time. But they never did.

Sure, his royalties weren't high anymore, but the amount would have covered the back charges for his apartment. With Arthur in his care now, he couldn't afford to lose this place. The bailiff had come twice already, but there was nothing valuable to seize. That didn't mean the management company was going to give up chasing him for the charges long overdue.

Could they really kick him out of his flat, with a child in his care?

Not so easily.

The winter was approaching too, and the law in France prohibited evictions in winter. Thank God, he had paid off this flat with his royalties from the good days. On top of all this, if he had a landlord after him for overdue rent, he would be in a real mess. That was the good side of things.

Now, if he could get through his interview this morning and land the job of concierge at the retirement home, he would be able to pay off the back charges before the end of this year.

The other interviewers had rejected him on the basis of either over or under qualification. The truth was: he had been out of the workforce for too long. In spite of his declining royalties, he never thought of enlisting with the employment office and looking for a job seriously—until Arthur came into his life. Now, at sixty two, he was too old to be hired even as a cashier at a supermarket.

But this job was different. The retirement home was in his town. People there knew about him and read his works. And the officer at the employment office had pulled her strings to arrange for this interview. Like her, he too was optimistic about the outcome, but he didn't want to start dreaming until he heard something positive from them.

Yet, like her, he too knew that it would be the perfect job for him.

Apart from sorting mails and answering phone and welcoming visitors, most of his workday would be spent sitting at the front desk—which meant he could devote himself to writing again.

The thought lifted his spirit and depressed it at the same time.

Lifted because, since Arthur came into his life, writing had taken on a new meaning for him, with a fresh surge of inspiration; depressed because, even if the book he was working on at this moment turned out to be as great as his first one, he couldn't have it published so easily, due to the horrible sales figures of his last three books.

But then, the real pleasure came not from publishing the book but from writing it. This concierge's job would give him just that precious opportunity for writing, with an unburdened mind.

François rolled the chair away from his desk and stood up. He needed to boost his energy before the interview. The best way for him to do that was through rigorous exercise. He put on his running shoes and left the building.

He crossed the market square, took the steep slope by the Town Hall and the medieval chateau, then joined the trail that led through the forest toward his favorite pond. The vineyards that lined the forest, the ones that were bursting with firm, ripe grapes only two weeks ago, now stood stripped.

The temperature had fallen by several degrees over the night. The air was chilly this morning. The fruits of late September had ripened already and permeated the air with their scents. A flock of swallows sat on the overhead electrical lines and chattered. Maybe they were arguing about whether to leave for Africa this year or not.

He heard the shrill quacks long before he reached the pond.

Steam fog rose from the water, veiled the ducks and the quails chasing each other on the surface. The frivolous climate had confused everyone this year. The birds that left for south were still here. And those that came from further north had already arrived. A fierce battle raged among them over territories. They didn't even notice François as he jogged past near them.

Then he saw the swan on the far bank; it had arrived early too. The large white bird sat on the edge of the water, bending its neck elegantly and cleaning the feathers on its back. François stopped. The swan saw him. It craned its neck, walked a few steps sideways, then plunged its head among the tall grass and rasped.

Another long neck rose from that patch of grass.

François gasped—the swan had a partner this year! For all these years he had been watching this swan, it came in autumn and left in spring, but always alone. All the other swans he had seen before lived in couples, but not this one.

From the gaits of the swan he knew the bird was old. Although he could never tell how old it was, until now he had thought it didn't take up a partner because of its age. But, for some reason, the swan had changed its mind this year.

The other swan looked much younger and agile; yet there was a matching grace in the gestures between the two, in sharp contrast with the other birds that rampaged over the water. The two swans completely ignored the battle that was going on around them. They seemed content just to be with each other, in that little circle of grass and watercress.

They didn't have a child to look after. At least, not yet.

François's chest tightened.

He forced his eyes away from the two swans. He couldn't deny his longings for feminine tenderness, but he also knew how cruel it would be to drag that young woman he liked in the middle of his troubles. Besides, partnership didn't come without a price.

And, as for Arthur, the boy was not a burden but blessing in his life.

His limbs felt lighter.

The veil of confusion and vulnerability lifted off him.

Suddenly, each tree along the far bank had a face, with a unique expression on it.

Yet, there was one commonality among them: they were happy just to be there on this earth.

And François realized, for the first time since he had been coming to this pond, that he was happy to be alive in this world with whatever little he had.

Now, each tree bathed its foliage under a liquid gold of light and smiled at him generously. He forgot his pains. He saw, no matter how harsh his struggle for survival had become, there were still rewards of living on this earth.

Subtle but tangible rewards.

The problem occurred when, compressed by his struggles, he ignored those rewards and focused only on his pains; when he allowed his mind to shrink—to such an extent that it sought relief by escaping into illusions. Now, just these few moments of respite in the nature had revived his spirit again, expanded his vision on life.

His battles still waited for him, but a grease of love had removed the squeaks from his living. He could see again that life was not *after* its struggles were over, but right now in the middle of them.

Not that he lacked the will to fight back.

Nor could he blame his struggles for the drop of his creativity.

On the contrary, it was those hardships that had revived his imagination lately, forced him to think out of the box again.

More than a decade ago, when his first book became an international hit, and his royalties came in by the truckloads, he had given up living and settled into a comfortable course of existing. That felt good for sometime, but then he started producing books that a writer addicted to comfort would produce. His next book still did reasonably well, but the two books after that barely gained a fourth in sales; and, when his last book didn't even earn back its advance, his publisher put him out on the street.

With the poor sales figures glaring on his forehead, no other publisher would risk their money on his works.

But all that changed after Arthur came into his life.

The battles that followed scraped away his comforts, brought back the sharp edge he had before. But what really helped was this: Arthur became an avid reader of his books. Now François had a demanding audience to satisfy at home, one that he also cared about the most. The manuscript he was working on changed its course suddenly, took on a punch he had never expected.

Struggles kept piling up for sure, but life became vivid and vigorous again.

A violent fight erupted between two male ducks. Each bird raised its trunk above the water, then slapped the other with its wings and tried to hold the other's head under the surface. François turned away from the pond. In this shifting climate for publishers and their shrinking pool of money, the fight among writers had become obscene too. But, right now, his first priority was to feed Arthur and keep a roof over his head.

Today's job interview was a crucial step in that direction. He rubbed his hands warm, and then ran back toward his town.

Arthur wasn't sure how Lutetia was going to pull off the trick with the cook, but she seemed perfectly at ease when Arthur entered the canteen. She noticed him right away and waved him over to the side of the serving counter. She opened a pastry box and held it before him.

"Will this work?"

The lemon cake was small, but Arthur could fit six candles on it. "Yes, thank you."

She closed the pastry box and handed it to Arthur. He glanced around, then quickly slid the box into his backpack.

"Don't worry about what others think." Lutetia reached over and touched his cheek. "You're doing this for a good reason."

Arthur nodded and moved away from the counter.

He was sure, if Lutetia knew how to cook, she would have made the cake herself, but maybe she was too young for that. She still lived with her parents in this town and went to the university in Paris. On her spare days, she worked at this canteen; yet somehow she found the time to read all the books written by Grandfather, and she loved every one of them.

Arthur had seen how her body tensed and how her eyes sparkled, when Grandfather came to the school to meet his teachers. She made every effort to stay near them, but Grandfather never took notice of her.

Or, if he did, he didn't consider a woman forty years younger appropriate for him.

That was a pity.

Lutetia was caring. She was mature enough to be the right woman for Grandfather. She certainly could have lessened his sufferings and guided him in situations where Arthur couldn't help. He wanted to talk to Grandfather about this, but he never had the courage.

Arthur joined the other kids in the queue and started thinking what he should write on the card he had made last night. Thibault saw him and came over.

"The English class is cancelled this afternoon."

"Why, the teacher is out sick again?"

"Yes, and for an indefinite period this time."

That was good. The kids didn't learn much from that teacher anyway, and the teacher knew that too. Besides, Arthur needed the afternoon to finish what he was doing—that was far more important to him than any class he knew.

They took their food and sat at a corner table. Soon other kids joined them, and they started betting on the soccer match that was taking place this weekend. With Thibault as their center forward, Arthur had no doubt their team would win. He had never seen another boy spin the football in the air like Thibault.

After school, Arthur returned home.

He hid the cake in his drawer, picked up his notes and Grandfather's manuscript, then left for the Town Library. The biology test was in two days, but he would prepare for it tomorrow. Before this evening, he needed to finish typing his remarks on the manuscript; he knew how important this new book was for Grandfather.

On the first floor, he sought out a quiet table and sat.

He spread his papers on the table and stared at his scribbled notes. He wondered where and how to begin his remarks. His scalp itched, and his limbs fidgeted. There were two empty bottles and a crushed soda can in the garbage bin under the table.

He was going to glance around, but then he remembered what Lutetia had said.

Without hesitating, he lifted the can and the two bottles from the bin, and put those inside his backpack. He was doing this for a good reason. Then he rose from his seat and went around the floor confidently. He checked the other bins as he went, but found no more cans or bottles.

He returned to his chair, sat before his notes, and still couldn't figure the best way to arrange his remarks.

He rose from his seat again.

He wandered through the library, through the aisles of literature for adolescents and young adults. He picked a book or two, read their back covers, and slid them back in their places. All these racks were full of protagonists that were either victims or escapists; he had grown sick of their stories.

Grandfather said: Literature is supposed to lift the mind.

But the books that the French teacher chose for their

class did just the opposite.

Particularly, the last book gave Arthur nightmares, made him throw up his meals. And he was not the only kid to have suffered those pangs. Some parents complained to the Principal of their school, but the French teacher defended his reading list saying those crimes were the realities of today, and the kids needed to be aware of those for their own safety.

The complaining parents never uttered a word after that.

When Arthur told Grandfather about that debate in their school, he didn't make a single comment; instead, he took Arthur to the National Library.

From the microfiche archive, he printed out old news clips, dating as far back as the nineteenth century. The same horrible crimes were committed against children in those epochs too; only the news didn't go around so widely and frequently then, as it happened over the internet today. The writers from those periods didn't paint a rosy world for children either; but they didn't exaggerate the crimes just to make their books sell.

That's where Grandfather's books differed from the rest.

The world in his stories was not painless for kids, but they didn't act like helpless complainers. His protagonists didn't sit around daydreaming or go around seeking vengeance. They strived and they thrived. If they perished, they went with dignity. When Arthur read Grandfather's books, he didn't pull the blanket over his head; he felt like going out and facing the world as it was.

But, at his school, they never read books like Grandfather's.

Didn't matter what the school forced him to read. Arthur believed in Grandfather's books.

In spite of all the difficulties Grandfather was going through these days, his new manuscript was a jewel.

Arthur had read it three times already. Each time, he had discovered something new in it to learn. That was why he had so much difficulty organizing his remarks. But, he absolutely needed to get his head in order and finish his feedback before Grandfather returned home this evening. That was the least Arthur could offer Grandfather on this special day.

Now he could see Grandfather in his chair, reading the feedbacks without a blink.

The vision cleared Arthur's mind. He returned to the table and focused on his notes.

François sat at the lounge of the psychiatric hospital, turning the pages of Marlene's medical documents the attendant had given him an hour ago.

His daughter's condition had deteriorated progressively over the past seven months. To keep up with that decline, the tranquilizers and the antidepressants had climbed up in their potencies; both the disease and its treatments had left their marks on her body. He could barely recognize his daughter in the last photo they had taken of her.

He closed his eyes and tried to imagine Marlene when she first showed up at his door, sixteen years ago. Apart from his angular features on the girl's chin and jaws, he really had the impression of seeing her Vietnamese mother standing before him. By then, Marlene had been in Paris for over a year already, working for an elite modeling company and struggling to survive in that cutthroat world.

The harsh battles had taken Marlene to the drugs. In spite of all his efforts at her rehabilitation, the girl firmly held on to her habits.

Her looks paid for those habits.

Her modeling career faded, and her agent started sending her out as hostess to the rich men traveling to the city. But, that too stopped when she became pregnant from one of her regulars and refused to abort the child.

The hospital attendant returned. Marlene had been moved out of the suicide prevention unit last night, but she wasn't in a condition to receive her father yet. François thanked the attendant, handed her back the medical file, and went out of the hospital.

He took the bus to the Montparnasse Station and waited for the suburban train that would take him to his town.

Kids from a Parisian school were leaving for a class by the sea somewhere in Brittany. The two educators kept shouting at the kids above their bustle and tried to keep them from wandering away. Children needed to travel for growth, but François had never been able to send Arthur to any educational trips. In spite of the subsidies they received from the Town Hall, those trips still remained too expensive for François to finance. Kids needed food in their stomach and a roof over their head before anything else.

Nevertheless, Arthur had grown incredibly in maturity.

The boy was at the top of his class and a legendary goalkeeper in his school.

And the robustness he had shown to François's growing financial difficulties could rarely be expected from a boy who was about to step into the uncertainties of teens. Since the court took away Arthur's parental authority from Marlene and handed it over to François, not once had he regretted having the boy around.

On the contrary, Arthur's presence had been his biggest source of joy, his biggest compensation for the struggles in life.

True, like Marlene, the boy was stubborn about his

ideas at times, and François needed to make sure the boy didn't go astray like his mother. But, not once had the boy done something that put François to shame.

The suburban train taxied at the platform. François entered the wagon and took the stairs to the upper floor. He sat by the window and tried to think what he was going to tell Arthur about Marlene.

The boy rarely asked any questions about his mother. If François started to talk about her, the boy stiffened. And the same desperate look returned to his face, one that François had seen four years ago when he went into the commissariat to take Arthur in his custody.

That look rekindled François's imagination about what the boy might have endured inside that locked apartment—when Marlene's first suicide attempt failed, and she lay unconscious for a day and a half, until a neighbor heard the boy whimpering and called the authorities. Those images were too painful for François; he avoided talking about Marlene to Arthur altogether.

The train dropped him at the station of his town. The gulp of fresh, herbaceous air cleared his head, stirred his appetite.

They had a meal at the church yesterday. The next meal was still a day away, but he knew the hunger would pass—its pangs were always the hardest the day after a meal.

The good side of hunger was: it stimulated his brain. He always worked better in empty stomach rather than full.

He entered his building and opened the mailbox. There were two letters, and both looked like bills.

One came from Arthur's school. It was the bill for his canteen for the next three months, which must be paid if Arthur was to keep eating his lunches there.

The other was the property tax for his apartment, due in two weeks. Words in stern, bold letters at the bottom reminded him of the steep fifteen percent penalty if the payment came in late. The State wasn't joking when they wrote that warning—François knew that from the one hundred sixty-two euros he had paid last year in penalty, for being only a day late.

He slid the two bills into the inside pocket of his jacket, then dragged his heels up the stairs to his apartment.

Arthur was waiting for him when he walked in through the door. The boy's eyes darkened as soon as he looked at Francois's face, but then they brightened again.

"Happy Birthday, Grandpa." He kissed François on the cheeks then moved to the door of the kitchen.

That's right! François had forgotten altogether.

There was a delicious cake on a saucer over the dinner table, with six blue candles on it. His throat twitched, and his eyes prickled. The boy must have saved all his pocket money to buy that cake.

"Thanks, Arthur."

François lowered his face, took off his shoes, and hung his coat on the door.

Arthur opened the fridge, poured the food from the church into a pan, and lightened the gas burner. François sat at the table.

"Heat enough for yourself only. I've had my dinner already."

"Did you?" The boy looked disappointed.

"We can share the cake, though."

There was an envelope under the saucer. François lifted the envelope and slid the folded paper out. There were only three lines on the sheet:

'You might have missed a book or two.
But you've written another great story again.
I'm sure you know that too.'

François didn't know how to deal with that message. He bit his lip and stared out the window. The setting sun painted the roof of the church yellow and red. A couple of storks coasted low over the roof then sat over the gable top.

"Let's pray, Grandpa."

Arthur had lit the candles, and now sat facing him.

"To God?" François shifted. "For my book?"

"Yes, let's do that."

"God has more important things to take care of."

"Helping us is not important?"

"God isn't there to provide us with unlimited charity."

"You never ask for charity!"

"We both know that's not true."

"Asking for child support from my father is not charity. Was that why you looked sad when you came in?"

"I'm not sad anymore."

"Did he promise to pay?"

"Arthur, it's a matter between adults."

"Did he at least reply?"

"Leave that to me."

"I don't want you to suffer because of me."

"It's a pleasure to have you around."

"I hope so, Grandpa."

"Here, I blow the candles out for you."

Arthur left the kitchen then returned with two pages, neatly typed.

He handed those pages to François. "Your surprise."

François knew what those pages were—he had seen his manuscript on Arthur's bedside table before. Yet, he couldn't help feeling overwhelmed.

He pretended he didn't know what those pages were

and started reading them.

"The best gift I can ever have, Arthur." He rose from the chair and drew the boy in his arms. "Your feedbacks are so much better than what I receive from editors."

The boy pressed his head on François's breastbone but said nothing.

"You believe what I said?"

The boy lifted his face and nodded. "When will this book come out?"

"I don't know. My publisher doesn't want anything from me."

"Take it to someone else then."

"I can't. I'm bound to them by an option clause."

"What's option clause?"

"They have the first right to look at my work."

"Did you show it to them?"

"I sent them the manuscript eight weeks ago."

"And?"

"Never heard back from them."

"That's awful." Arthur broke away from his arms and started pacing the room. "They never even pay you on time."

François startled. But then, Arthur's knowledge wasn't a surprise.

The boy, however, didn't know the course of François's relationship with his publisher.

In the past, when his books were selling hot, they always paid him on time. Now, he had to wait until the bestselling authors received their checks first. That was his publisher's strategy to survive in this shaky, low margin business; François could perfectly understand them. In their place, he would have done the same probably.

Arthur stopped pacing. "Don't you say we always have to be fair?"

"Sure."

"Your publisher has broken his promise. You can break yours too."

"That's not the way fairness should work, Arthur."

But the boy's remark made François think.

There might be a way out of this impasse and allow his manuscript a second chance. Given the way his publisher had acted until now, this new path wouldn't be entirely unfair to them.

François placed his hands over the boy's shoulders. "Let's try your cake."

The sun had crossed over the church when François finished the final changes to his manuscript. He printed out a fresh copy, then sat down thinking about the ethicality of what he was about to do.

Legally, the option clause in the contract with his

current publisher required him to wait for a definite rejection of his new manuscript by them, before he could show it to another publisher.

But, also legally, his current publisher had broken the terms of their contract by not paying his legitimate royalties on time, and by not providing him a detailed account for the sales of his backlist books.

Ethically, he had been right by giving them the first chance to read his new manuscript, and they had been wrong by maintaining complete silence about it, not even acknowledging its reception.

Also, ethically, it was his responsibility to square his own finances and protect Arthur in his charge, by publishing this manuscript—particularly when his instincts told him that the novel was good, and he could make honest money from it by going with this new publisher he had been thinking about.

There was no guarantee that this new publisher would act any differently from his current one in the long term. But, for now, the Chief Editor of this new publisher he was going to meet this afternoon had been an enthusiastic reader of his books. She knew about his poor sales over the last years, yet she respected his works for their high literary quality.

She seemed humane too, when he talked to her on the phone.

In her hands, his new manuscript would have the best

chance for publishing, with the due care it deserved.

He was ethically right in giving her a physical copy of his manuscript, but he needed to make sure words didn't go around about it—he didn't need a lawsuit from his current publisher on top of everything else he had on his back. He also needed to make sure he kept the trails of all communications with his current publisher.

He tidied up his desk then left for the public library of his town.

He opened his email at the internet terminal, created a separate folder and moved all his communications with the current publisher into that folder, then sent their commissioning editor another reminder for his overdue royalties and asking for feedback on the new manuscript he had sent nine weeks and two days ago. Then he printed out a list of antique bookshops and pawn shops in Paris, and returned to his apartment.

One by one, he loaded his reference books in the duffle bag, then kneeled beside them and sighed.

That's alright. He didn't use those books often anymore.

He stood up and looked around his shelves, but he couldn't find anything else that would have any market value for sale. He opened the drawer and pulled out the gold-embroidered case—his father's writings were still visible on its back. He took out the fountain pen and rolled it over his palm—his father's words still sounded in his ears.

His lips quivered and his fingers trembled. He replaced the pen inside its case, slid it inside the drawer, and shut it quickly.

He carried the bag of books out of his apartment and closed the door. He stood with his forehead over the pane and shut his eyes.

He was being stupid to hold onto souvenirs when the basic needs were at stake.

Besides, he treasured that fountain pen so much that, until now, he had never used it even once. Maybe, unconsciously, he had saved the pen for such an occasion. Moreover, if his father knew the reason for selling the pen today, he would certainly applaud François from his tomb.

He opened the door and took the pen out of the drawer.

He took the suburban train to Saint-Michel Notre Dame, where he traded his books and pen. The four hundred sixty-nine euros would cover the canteen bill for Arthur plus the property tax, and would leave him a few euros in change. He took the cash to the post office on the square, deposited it into his account, and mailed the checks for the bills.

There was still one hour and forty minutes to go before his meeting with the Chief Editor of the new publishing house.

He stopped before a street-side vendor of warm sandwiches, slid his hand inside the pocket for money, but then remembered that the church was providing a meal tonight. He could hold back his tongue until then. Arthur could use those spare changes to buy his school supplies. He was amazed how the boy could get by with so little for everything he needed.

Sometimes François wondered if someone in the school or in the town was giving money to Arthur, but he couldn't think of a discreet way of asking the boy without hurting his feelings.

At the same time, Arthur had dignity. François couldn't see the boy accepting money or any other favor from someone.

His mobile phone rang when he was strolling around Pantheon. The call came from the woman at the employment office. François's face tingled. He pressed the answering button and stepped into a quieter alley.

"Can we talk now?" the woman said.

"Sure."

"I've some news for the post of concierge." She paused. "Sorry I couldn't get back to you before."

François didn't like her pause; his fingertips went cold.

"They really enjoyed meeting you."

He relaxed his grip on the phone. "That's good."

"But they're looking for someone below forty-five."

François was stunned. The job wasn't that physical. At sixty-two, he still had everything that the work demanded.

"I know how you feel, but their decision has to do with—"

"The State's employment legislation."

"Right. An employee of your age can't be fired easily."

His face became hot. A curse almost escaped his mouth, but he bit his lip.

Anyway, he didn't want to work for an employer who worried about firing an employee before hiring. At the same time, he couldn't deny what the employment officer was hinting at: he was only three years away from the legal retirement age.

He thanked her for the efforts and slid the phone into the breast pocket of his coat.

His legs felt numb; and his chest, hollow. He trudged to the fountain and sat on its border. There was no way for him to find a job at this age.

The meeting with the Chief Editor of the new publisher was in twenty-five minutes. Being in this mood wasn't going to help him for that meeting, and sitting disheartened like this wasn't going to help him lift his mood. He stood up. His head spun; dark spots clouded his vision. He ignored his low blood sugar and kept walking toward Place d'Odeon.

The Chief Editor had arrived at the café before time—that was a good sign. François greeted her on the cheeks and sat at the table.

"Thanks for coming."

"Thanks for letting me have a look at your work."

"Here it is." François put the manuscript on the table. "An unofficial copy."

"I'm taking it straight home. There won't be any talks about this in my office."

"How long do you need?"

"Two weeks." She sized the manuscript. "Maybe three."

"How is life at office?"

"You know all that, don't you?"

"I hope this manuscript doesn't disappoint you."

"Your books never disappoint me."

"We can't be so sure."

"You're confusing quality with sales."

"Quality doesn't survive without sales."

She exhaled. "Come on! Don't pretend you know nothing about the industry of publishing."

"The taste of readers has changed."

"The taste of readers has been rigged to change."

"What difference does it make at the end?"

"The impact of a great story has remained unchanged."

François lowered his eyes. "Age has weakened my storytelling."

"No. Age has strengthened your spirit."

"I don't see the connection."

"One needs a great spirit to tell a great story."

Afterward, they walked along the banks of Seine up to Place des Invalides.

Then François took the suburban train back to his town. He didn't want to go back to his apartment immediately, so he took the small streets around the town, thinking about what the Chief Editor had said since they left the café.

He was shocked at first.

Then he could believe what she said about the publishers: they needed their authors not to challenge the readers, but to confirm the beliefs the readers already held. That was the most effective way of winning readers and boosting sales.

But, for her, the problem was: writers like François never saw their purpose of writing from this point of view. They only wrote what they felt they had to write.

She was right on both accounts, but neither helped François really.

At least her arguments explained why the literary market today was choked with gruesome murderers, lonesome victims, and wild-eyed fantasists. Her points also made it clear why a publisher, even if they chose to ignore his poor track record, would not dare to buy his protagonist and his story.

He couldn't persuade the publishers to change their point of view. On his side, he couldn't force himself to see life differently either.

How could he write something he didn't believe in?

How could he depict an emotion he hadn't experienced himself?

How could he create a pathetic protagonist when he, himself, had never felt pathetic in life?

In spite of all his hardships, he had never felt like a victim.

Nor alone.

The hand of the Universe had been present in his life all along.

He never uttered a word of prayer, but he had always seen that invisible cooperation from the Universe: whenever he put in his best efforts, along with the best intentions and the best principles in mind, the right collaboration always showed up at the right place and at the right time.

When he wrote this new book, that's exactly what he had done.

That was why the Universe had collaborated with him again, by placing the Chief Editor of this new publisher on his path.

So, this had to be the sign that this new book would work out fine.

He had wandered through the park without knowing, and now he stood before his building. He walked in through the front door and opened the mailbox: there was only one letter today, and it looked like another bill.

No, it wasn't a bill.

It was a letter from the company of electricity and gas. The legal words, polite but firm, informed him that, if the overdue bills weren't paid within two weeks, the supplies would be cut.

He shoved the letter into his pocket and tried to recall the compliments the Chief Editor had given him on his books. Arthur was about to return from school, and François needed to cheer himself up before that.

The teacher handed out the exam schedule and asked the class to be careful about what had happened last year around this time.

Arthur knew the same would happen this year too—he had seen the firecrackers and the paintballs in the locker room—but what bothered him more was the group of kids from the neighboring town that hung out near the gate at school breaks, with beer cans in their hands. Thibault was beginning to lose patience with them, and one only needed a small cause to start a big fight these days.

Arthur checked out the practice tests from his school's library, then headed across the yard toward the gate. His classmates were already on the soccer field—the announcement of the exams might have sent them there earlier today—but Thibault wasn't among them. Lutetia had finished her work at the canteen and was now unlocking her scooter near the guard's lodge. She noticed Arthur and called him over.

"You need a ride?"

"No, thanks." He did want to ride her scooter, but the problem was: she didn't have an extra helmet. If he fell, it would cost Grandfather money.

"How were classes?"

"Fine."

"How is your grandfather's new book coming up?"

"Great."

Lutetia waited for more. Then she raised her eyebrows and drove away.

Arthur did want to tell her more about the book, but he didn't really know how things were coming along for it.

Lately, he had seen Grandfather more bogged down than usual. There was a new editor in the scene now, and Grandfather spoke highly of her, but, somehow his enthusiasm seemed overpowered by a looming sense of anxiety, and Arthur couldn't figure out whether it was because of this new editor or their strained finances.

The kids from the neighboring town were taunting a boy near the bus stop—it wasn't Thibault or anyone Arthur knew from his school. He avoided that route and took the street by the supermarket.

Even though Grandfather never treated him like a burden, Arthur knew his presence didn't make Grandfather's life any easier. He wished Grandfather were more demanding with people who owed him money. He wished Grandfather were tougher with others in general, the way he was with Arthur sometimes.

But, no.

Grandfather always chose to see things from the perspective of others, before he saw things from his own.

Others, of course, never acted so generously with Grandfather.

He couldn't change Grandfather. The only thing he could do was to excel at his exams and win the scholarship at school. The amount was only one thousand euros, but it would still be a contribution to their household.

He could imagine Grandfather's poised pride when Arthur brought home the news of his scholarship. Didn't matter what the other kids said about his abandoning the soccer team these days. Things always had to be done in the right order of priority—that's a valuable lesson he had learnt by watching Grandfather.

Smell of delicious pastries filled his nostrils and flooded his mouth. He turned his face away from the baker's shop and kept walking. The two coins in his pocket would serve better to buy the book he needed for a class.

Arthur entered their apartment.

He was hoping to see Grandfather at his desk, but he wasn't there.

Over these last days, Grandfather had been spending more and more time outside their apartment. Certainly, being outside reminded him less of the weight he had to carry on his shoulders.

The apartment had picked up the smell of an odd emptiness too.

Odd—not because the valuables had disappeared one by one, but because it felt like a place its dweller was no longer connected to.

Arthur remembered the seaside hotel he had been to with Grandfather long ago. He remembered how, on the morning of their departure, they both stood looking at the sea from their window; then how they packed up and left their room without looking back once.

Lately, when he found Grandfather looking out the

window of their apartment, he saw the same detachment on his face.

And that made Arthur afraid.

This was the only secure place for Arthur on earth. He couldn't imagine his life without this place or without Grandfather.

Before, he had heard about the horror stories in the orphan homes owned by the State. He had spent sleepless nights worrying about those homes, until the court granted his parental authority to Grandfather. Even after that, the nightmares took several weeks to go away.

But, why was he thinking about those now?

Because, he was being lazy.

Whereas Grandfather was out somewhere fighting for his book, here was Arthur postponing his revision for exams by indulging in dark memories. Whereas Grandfather struggled on to keep their boat floating, here was Arthur worrying about what would happen to him if the boat sank.

He couldn't imagine anyone he could have inherited this selfishness from; so, it had to be his own make. He gathered his books and sat at Grandfather's desk to study.

He couldn't.

He opened the window and looked across the train station.

He looked over the poplars and the maples and the

oaks that lined the tracks, and then at the top of the church that fed them three meals a week and clothed them through the seasons.

Their situation was sad, but the sight somehow inspired him and lightened his heart. The same must happen to Grandfather too, when he looked out the window.

True, recently Grandfather had been more serious and intense than usual.

But, wasn't Arthur the same way when he had to prepare for an important exam?

This new novel was highly important to Grandfather.

Probably, what he had seen on Grandfather's face was not detachment but concentration. Grandfather could be thinking about his novel when he looked out this window.

The novel was important to Arthur too, but not for the same reason.

Unlike the other novels of Grandfather, Arthur had a personal stake in this book. He could identify himself better with its protagonist and see events in his own life under a different light. That helped him understand the significances of everything that had happened to him. Now, he could not only look at this world more positively, but also lift the regard he had toward himself.

No other book had done this for him before.

He could never know for sure, but somehow he felt

that his presence might have pushed Grandfather to build this new protagonist. If that were indeed the case, Arthur's life would have added some value to Grandfather. And, if the book succeeded, it might even pull them out of their financial troubles.

Now he felt much better.

But, a new worry pressed down upon him: he absolutely wanted this novel to succeed. Yet, he knew he couldn't do anything more about it.

He returned to his desk and opened his exercise book. Only two pages were left in it, and there wasn't a new one on his shelf. The change in his pocket wouldn't buy him a new notebook. He took the keys of the cellar, closed the apartment, and went down the stairs.

He took the two canvass bags out of the cellar and carried them upstairs. They were untouched; Grandfather never went down to the cellar.

He left the building with the two bags on his shoulders and started climbing the slope toward the supermarket. As usual, people glanced at him and raised their eyebrows, but that didn't matter to him anymore.

He was doing this for a good reason.

As he walked in through the sliding doors of the supermarket, the woman at the help desk saw him and came out smiling.

Together, they counted the cans and the bottles. Then she handed him twelve euros and seventy cents in change. Arthur bought three notebooks and a set of pens; those would do till Christmas.

As he was going down the street by the church, someone called out his name.

It was Thibault! His one eye was black, but the other glittered. He held a soccer ball in one hand and a long chocolate bar in the other.

Arthur went to the soccer field with Thibault. Studies could wait till evening.

François's mobile rang. He switched on the bedside lamp and reached for the phone. The hospital was calling: Marlene had locked herself in the toilet and sliced her wrist. She was found in a pool of blood half an hour ago.

François rolled out of the bed and slid into his pants. He stopped at the door of Arthur's room—the boy still slept with that blissful smile on his face. He started to write a note for him, but then tore it off. The boy would know where his grandfather had gone; this was not the first time François had to leave for the hospital in the middle of the night. Besides, there was no need to torment the boy before the severity of his mother's condition was known.

François swung his coat over the shoulder, pulled the

door behind him gently, and rushed out of the building.

For Marlene's funeral, François sold the necklace he had received from his mother. He had kept the necklace hidden until now—he was supposed to give it to Marlene in case she ever married—and now it paid for her funeral.

With what was left after paying the undertaker, he cleared off his overdue life insurance premium, then went to the post office to pay his gas and electricity bills. The postal clerk handed him a packet of letters for Marlene, forwarded from her address at the hospital.

She had left Arthur with no assets but a mountain of debts.

The girl was bankrupt, and this might have been the real reason for her suicide. Surprisingly, the boy had taken his mother's death well: after two days of complete silence, he started to resume his life slowly and came back to almost normal. Now, this was not the way for Arthur to start the finances of his life.

François came out of the post office and sat on a bench under the redwood tree. He took out his pen and started calculating the total amount of money Arthur would receive, in case his grandfather died.

Arthur was his only legal heir now. Yet, the tax rate that would apply when he inherited anything from his grandfather would not be the one that Marlene would have paid but its double. Given the running market value of his flat, that inheritance tax bill would amount to about sixty thousand euros.

The State, however, wouldn't tax the money from the insurance François had taken on his life. Arthur being the sole beneficiary of that insurance, he would receive the full one hundred fifty thousand euros into his account. After paying off the inheritance tax and the debts left by Marlene, the boy would still have some seventy thousand euros to go on with. But then, the creditors of Marlene wouldn't leave Arthur in peace until his grandfather died, and the boy recovered all that money.

Right now, François couldn't die either.

At this moment, Arthur needed his grandfather more alive than dead. The boy was talented; he needed to survive and have a decent chance at life. François was sure God would be fair enough to give the boy that chance.

For him, God was not superior to Man. If Man needed God to do his work, God also needed Man to do His work right. The boy showed all the promises to make a difference in this world, so there was every reason for God to collaborate with him.

For now, they just needed to survive one day at a time and take things as they came.

François was about to leave for the employment bureau when his phone rang. The Chief Editor of the new publishing house was calling. He took off his shoes and sat at the desk.

"Sorry I didn't call you before," she said. "I had to read your manuscript twice all over."

"How did you feel about it?"

"This one is your masterpiece."

François closed his eyes and took in a deep breath. "Thank you."

"You'll pardon me, but I had to speak with my boss about your manuscript." She paused. "Rest assured, he has promised me, the words will not go around."

"What did he say?"

"We'll make you an offer."

She gave him the amount. François gasped—the amount was five times more than what he had received from his current publisher for his last book. He didn't know how to react.

"Has your publisher refused the manuscript?"

"Not yet." Fifteen weeks had elapsed since he emailed the manuscript to them and never received a response. "We can take their no news as good news for us."

"Are you willing to work with me?"

"What kind of a question is that?"

"See if you can get an answer from them."

"I'll try."

After they hung up, François paced the room. He had sent at least a dozen emails to the commissioning editor of his current publisher, called him at least a hundred times, but all that had been of no use. It was as if the commissioning editor had left the publishing house, but François knew he still worked for them.

There was an hour and half before the employment office would close for lunch. François sat at his desk again and stared at his phone. He fidgeted for a few moments, fiddled with the phone in his hand, then called the commissioning editor of his current publisher.

By magic, the editor picked up the phone. "Yes?"

"Good Morning, it's François."

"I know."

"Have you had a chance to read the manuscript?"

"The Financial Director is looking at it."

"Pardon me?"

"He is the one who makes the final decision."

"Since when?"

"Are you willing to publish it under a pseudonym?"

"Why?" François couldn't believe his ears. "Are you making babies these days under a pseudonym too?" He regretted the slip of his tongue; this was not the time to return an insult.

"Look, your sales have been horrible, and no bookseller will take up a new title from you under your real name."

"Thanks, but the answer is—"

François realized he was going to make another mistake, so he stopped. There are times when head has to take priority over heart, and this was one of those. He inhaled deeply and exhaled.

"I need some time to think over."

"Alright then." The editor hung up.

François went to the bathroom and splashed cold water over his face. That cooled the heat, but didn't calm his head. The apartment suffocated him now. He went to the park and sat on a bench.

He started weighing the two choices before him.

The relation with the commissioning editor of his current publisher had already been spoilt for years now. But, the fact that this editor proposed the route of a pseudonym meant he had at least skimmed through the manuscript; and the fact that he had passed it to their Financial Director meant they had at least some interest in the book. If François chose to go by a pseudonym for this book, contractually this publisher would be required to make an offer at least as good as their last offer, and their new advance would pay off the back charges for his apartment. Their fresh interest in his new manuscript might even incite them to pay his overdue royalties too.

On the other hand, if he refused to take the route of pseudonym, and his current publisher refused to publish his new manuscript, he would be free to go with the new publisher. Their Chief Editor would need some time to sort things out with their contract department, but, given the chemistry between him and her, she would do everything in her power to speed up the process.

Besides, with his current publisher, there was no guarantee yet that they would publish this manuscript. Even if they did, there was no guarantee they would hurry to offer him a new contract and pay the advance quickly. Certainly his commissioning editor there was not going to push them for any of this. More François thought, more the route of his current publisher looked like a dead end to him.

On the contrary, the route of the new publisher looked like a highway in the open.

Most of all, François wanted to take responsibility for what he wrote. Publishing under his real name would allow him to preserve his integrity and dignity. So there could be no ambiguity about his choice. He left the park, went to the Town Library, and sent an email to the commissioning editor of his current publisher.

He was refusing to publish his new manuscript under a pseudonym.

The doorbell rang. François rolled away from the desk and opened the door. The bailiff stood on the landing, with a letter in his hand.

"Court order." He handed the letter to François and took out a folded sheet from his bag.

"Order for what?"

"I don't know." He unfolded the sheet and pointed to a space with François's name. "Please sign here."

François signed the acknowledgement receipt, then closed the door and opened the envelope. In fifteen days, he was required to appear before the civil court, in order to defend his case for not having paid the charges for his apartment. The management company had sued him before the court. Sweat dripped from under his armpits, and his tongue stuck to the palate. He gulped down two glasses of water, then clutched the glass to his throbbing chest. Panic was not going to help him now.

Maybe it was the best that the management company had assigned him before the court. It would be easier to argue his case before a judge than before the heartless folks in that company. Besides, there were quite a few items on the list of charges that seemed unclear or downright unfair, and this would be the time to bring all this out before the court.

Maybe, after all, this lawsuit was a blessing in disguise.

He took the court papers to his desk and started reading them line by line. His back charges reported by the management company seemed accurate, but a hefty amount of legal expenses had been added to them, which he would have to pay if he lost the case. Given the way the management company ran this building, there was little chance for them to win.

Of course, the management company had not provided the court any details on that dubious renovation fund, which was established five years ago, and which was still collecting money from the owners of the apartments. To date, their building hadn't seen the slightest hint of improvement; but the provision for renovation accounted for almost a third of the total charges that the owners had to pay.

The justice system in France was not yet a financial muscle flexing contest between the plaintiff and the defendant. No fair judge, in a clear state of mind, would let the management company get away with those huge anomalies of unexplained charges.

The letter prevented François from selling the flat without permission from the court, but selling had never really been an option for him for various reasons.

True, by selling the flat, he could have paid off those back charges, and still would be left with some good savings in the bank; but, afterward, nobody would rent him a flat in the private rental market, because his annual income was too low.

He could qualify for low income housing, but, even for those flats, the lowest rent was seven hundred euros a month, and the minimum waiting time was a year and a half.

He could have bought a smaller flat in a cheaper neighborhood farther away from Paris, but that meant Arthur would lose his friends and start all over again. After those instabilities the boy had been through for his age, he really needed this stability for now to grow.

The letter advised him that he might be able to get a free lawyer from the State to defend his case, and an annexed document laid out the conditions he would need to meet in order to procure that service. The total of his unemployment benefits would have qualified him for that service, but the market value of his flat disqualified him altogether.

He set the court documents aside and paced the apartment.

He looked out the window, tried to recall his last conversation with the Chief Editor of the new publishing house. On that occasion, he informed her about that email he had sent to the commissioning editor of his current publisher, refusing to publish the manuscript under a pseudonym, and gave her his feelings about the consequences he expected to follow from his refusal. She was highly optimistic about the outcomes then.

He returned to his desk and called the Chief Editor. Within two rings, she picked up the phone.

"I was just going to call you."

The tone of her voice alarmed him. "About what?"

"I talked with our contracts department, and they need a formal release from your current publisher."

"Their option clause has expired."

"I know. They can still change their mind and match our offer at the last moment."

"Are your people being paranoid?"

"Apparently, that's how it works in publishing."

François sighed. "So what do you need from me exactly?"

"A formal refusal. An email will work."

"I'll see what I can do."

There was no way he could get a definite refusal from his current publisher, not if they had seen the slightest potential for the manuscript; even less, if they felt he was taking it to another publisher.

And they would know if he pushed for a formal refusal.

Time was up for polite requests; he was going to act tough-handed now. He closed his apartment and left for the Town Library.

He wrote an email to the commissioning editor of his

current publisher: the option clause had expired, and, by not responding within the contractually specified time, they had forfeited their rights to publish this manuscript.

He wanted to add an argument for the unpaid royalties too, but then decided to save it for later. Only the expiration of the option clause would suffice for what he needed.

He sent the email and printed out a copy.

Emails were considered official these days, but, just to be safe, he would send a hard copy of the notice to his current publisher by registered post, with an acknowledgement receipt. That would cost him a few euros, but the money was worth spending.

Against the avalanche of legalese brought down by the lawyer of the management company, François defended his case before the civil court by himself—using simple, humane language.

At the end, the judge ruled: François wasn't required to reimburse the management company for their legal expenses, but he was required to pay, within six months, the part of the back charges that was not due to the provision for renovation. Given his current situation, he could pay this net overdue amount in three installments, the first of which was to be paid by the end of next month.

And, although it was not part of this particular case,

the judge also ordered that, until the management company convened with the co-owners and agreed upon the details of the plan for refurbishment, the co-owners would stop contributing to the fund for renovation.

Both rulings seemed fair to François, but now he was left with the burden of paying six hundred seventy eight euros by next month's end.

Nevertheless, it was a small victory.

After he left the court and returned to his town, he treated himself to a nice run around his favorite pond and came back to his apartment with fresh energy.

His contract with the new publisher would be signed soon; and his advance, paid. After he sent that registered letter to his current publisher three weeks ago, he called the Chief Editor of the new publisher. She assured him their contract department would be able to use a copy of that letter as a proof of refusal by his current publisher, in case he didn't hear back from them within a reasonable time.

Until last Friday, he hadn't heard anything from his old publisher that would make him believe the contrary.

He took a cold shower then left for the Town Library. His new publisher would need some information on him to draw up their contract, and it was easier to give that information over email than phone. Besides, now that the option clause with his old publisher had expired, he could officially communicate with his new publisher by written means.

He sat before the terminal and opened his email.

His heart jumped: there was an email from the commissioning editor of his old publisher. It was sent this morning when he was at the court. Maybe it was some frustrated remark from this editor; given his character, François wouldn't rule out such a response from him. With quivering hands, he clicked on the email.

The message was only one line. The commissioning editor was informing François that eight more weeks still remained for their option clause to expire.

François's head spun; his limbs went numb. He was sure the commissioning editor was wrong. The option clause was valid only for three months, and that period ended five weeks ago. He closed his email and ran back to his flat.

He scrounged through his binder and found his copy of the contract he had signed with them for his last book. He flipped through the pages, came to the section of the option clause, and his eyes started to blur.

The commissioning editor was right: the option clause was still valid for two more months.

He dropped the binder on the floor and sat against the wall.

Could this have been a mistake by their contract

department?

He doubted that.

Anyway, whose mistake it was didn't matter at this point. The contract had been endorsed and signed by François, and that was all that mattered as far as the law was concerned.

He reached for the binder, took out the contracts for all his books with this publisher, and compared the option clauses in them. The first two had duration of three months, whereas the rest had been increased to six. Otherwise, the contracts were identical. Since he was satisfied with the wordings of the first two contracts, he must have stopped reading the next ones word by word.

Meanwhile, the noose of the option clause had tightened around his neck.

He was at fault here, not his publisher. Technically, they could make him wait for eight more weeks, and he could do nothing about it. He needed to let the new publisher know this as soon as possible, but he was not in a state to do that right now.

For the first time in life, François felt really desperate. He didn't want Arthur to see him in this state, but he didn't know how to calm himself down before the boy returned from school.

He dumped the binder on his desk and ran out of the building.

François sold the last of his possessions. He still needed two hundred fifty four euros more before the end of the week.

For three dawns, he stood in file with the day laborers on the footbridge over the railway tracks in his town, but none of the trucks hired him. He couldn't blame them: he was too old for that kind of work. Besides, over the last weeks, he had lost a considerable amount of his muscle mass.

He called the blood banks to sell his blood. He found out that the amount of blood he would require to sell to earn that much money was nearly twice the legal amount he could sell at once. Given his age and his current impoverished state, he wasn't sure he could even sell the legal amount to them.

He couldn't beg that money from anyone he knew.

That left him with only one solution.

After a few calls around, he found one clinic in the market district of a big neighboring town, where they paid cash for blood and didn't even ask the seller's name. The price, of course, was lower than what they paid in the legal market. François knew he was taking a risk, but then people didn't die unless they lost a huge amount of blood. Even though the clinic was illegal, they wouldn't take so much blood from him as to hemorrhage him to death—that would certainly get them in trouble.

He didn't know how he could cover the other two installments, but he would worry about that later. The Chief

Editor of the new publisher said there were ways to buy out the contract from his old publisher. That could work but not immediately. Meanwhile, he had to pay this installment by the end of the week and avoid being in the bad books of the court.

He put on his jacket and left for the neighboring town.

The clinics were required to provide food after drawing blood, to boost the seller's glucose level—but not the illegal ones. François took the cash, hid it in the breast pocket of his coat, then staggered out of the building.

On the streets, people took him for drunk and moved out of his way.

Within a block, he felt he was going to swoon, and started seeing floaters in his vision. He tumbled into an alley, grabbed the gutter pipe of a building, and lowered himself to the ground. His heart fluttered. He knew the malaise would pass, if he rested for a few minutes. He leaned his back against the wall and closed his eyes.

When he opened his eyes again, he was lying on the ground.

He sat up in panic and shoved his hand inside the coat; his wallet and phone were gone. His brain squirmed, he felt like he was going to pass out again. He grabbed the pipe, pulled himself up to his feet, then started walking out of the alley.

He dug his hand inside a garbage bin, pulled out a

half-eaten banana and a partially empty bottle of coke, and started devouring those.

People stared at him with disdain—his hair and clothes were soiled by now—but the social mirrors didn't matter to him anymore. All he cared for was to get back to his town before it was too late. There was a meal at the church tonight, and he didn't want the boy to miss that food.

But, he needed a train ticket to get back to his town.

At the station, he approached the ticket counter, and explained his situation to the woman behind the glass. She looked him up and down, then narrowed her eyes.

"So what do you expect me to do?"

"Would you kindly allow me to take the train?"

"We don't let people travel for free."

"I promise to pay back, Madame. It's only three stations."

"We don't let people travel on credit either."

A queue of tourists had already formed behind him. "Please, Madame. I have a child at home, and I must get back on time."

"That's your problem, not mine."

"Would you please speak to your manager?"

"Stand aside please, thank you."

He could travel without a ticket.

But, this town being a favorite tourist destination,

there were many ticket controllers in the trains and on the platforms. If he were caught without a ticket, without any money and identity card on him, he would go straight to the commissariat of police and spend the night in detention.

On the other hand, his town was only twelve kilometers away through the forest—he had jogged a couple of times on that forest trail before. If he left now, he could be in his town in three hours at the maximum. The church would still be open for food.

He needed to let Arthur know somehow, but there was no way. The landline at his home had been cut long ago, and he couldn't afford a mobile phone for the boy. He could call a neighbor, but he didn't know their numbers. Even if he did, his phone was stolen. From the way he looked now, people would never trust him with their phones. He left the station and started walking along the boulevard, toward the intersection where the entrance of the trail through the forest was.

He left the busy boulevard and entered the forest.

His mind calmed somewhat.

The cold air refreshed his face. The smell of decomposing leaves permeated the forest. The sun had set long ago, but the winter birds still chirped on the naked branches. Farther he moved into the forest, deeper he felt immersed into the movements and sounds of the evening. His heart stopped fluttering; its rhythm synchronized with the vibes around him.

Little by little, he forgot the harsh treatments he had received from people and embraced the loving grace from his surroundings.

He arrived at the plateau overlooking the valley. He drank from a natural spring he knew, then felt tired and sat on a rock. A layer of fog swept gently over the silhouettes of the trees below him and made the place look surreal. Almost like a fairyland.

Life always came with its magic.

But, to attend that magic show, he had to sustain life.

When he was young, he wanted life's magic but didn't want to pay its price. Then, as he progressed in age, he learnt to be fair. He accepted life's costs, along with the benefits it brought.

He saw senses didn't exist without life. He couldn't expect his sensorial organs to feel life's pleasures only, and not its pains. Senses simply didn't work that way.

A fox howled from below.

He rose from the rock and started descending into the valley. His body shook, and an electric spark ran through his head. He grabbed the trunk of a tree and steadied himself. His blood sugar was low, but he had already crossed a third of his path; in two more hours, he would reach his town. His heart fluttered again, and his eyes blurred, but he ignored those malaises and trudged down the trail.

Fog had thickened over the bottom of the valley.

The trail forked ahead, and he couldn't remember which branch led to his town. He searched around the intersection, but couldn't find a sign anywhere. He knew that one branch continued through the forest, whereas the other went to a town nearby. He needed to take the branch away from that town to get to his.

The fox howled again, but from his left this time.

He took that call as a sign: the branch that went to his town had to be on the left.

The left trail soon narrowed and passed through a part of the forest he had never seen before. His breath labored, and his limbs trembled. He still forged ahead, convinced that this was the right path and he didn't recognize it in darkness and fatigue.

But, when he reached a busy departmental road, he knew he was not in the direction of his town.

He looked behind. There was no trace of the trail or any other path. For all this time, he might have just wandered through the forest; it would be impossible now to find his way back through those trees.

He stood by the side of the road, stretching his arm out and holding up his thumb.

Not a vehicle stopped or slowed down. He couldn't blame them. In their place, if he saw a ragged man asking for a lift in the middle of a forest, he would have done the same.

The fox howled from the back.

He lowered his arm and went back through the trees, in a direction he thought he might have come from.

He stopped before a house that looked like a chateau.

Now he knew he was lost—there was no chateau on the way to his town.

Yet, the façade of the chateau looked oddly familiar.

On the signing tours for his first book, he had been to a few chateaus. But that was more than a decade ago, and he couldn't remember if this chateau was one of those. From where he stood, its outer rooms looked dark. Even if there were light in there, he wouldn't dare knocking on their door, with his current look and without his identity card on him.

He waited for the fox to howl, but it didn't anymore.

He must have left the forest long back somewhere and entered the woods. The low blood sugar was seizing his head and limbs again; he needed to move. He followed a narrow path that went along the outer wall of the chateau through the bushes and reached a clearing.

Smell of ripe oranges flooded his nose. His tongue watered, his stomach writhed. A garden lay at the far end of the chateau, and the wind brought the smell from there. His whole body turned against his will and led his feet toward the source of that smell.

Orange trees, in this part of France?

Yes. He wasn't hallucinating.

A low wall separated the orchard from the woods. Beyond that wall, crescent moon shivered over a rectangular reservoir of water, and the orange trees lined its four sides.

Ripe oranges hung low on his side of the reservoir.

If he climbed on that wall, he might be able to reach those fruits. He had never stolen anything from anyone before, but now he needed a few of those oranges to boost his blood sugar and find his way back home. The chateau looked closed and deserted from here; there was little chance of being caught by anyone at this moment.

He gathered his courage and stepped toward the wall. His legs trembled, and his head buzzed. He scrambled up the wall and sat on its top. One branch hung within his reach, and he saw the fruits on it were not oranges but Corsican clementines.

Then he saw the fox.

The animal stood under a tree and looked straight at him.

Its burning eyes were frozen in fear, as if the fox was asking him to give up what he was doing and go back. That would be stupid, especially when the fruits were so easy to grab. He brushed his doubts aside and stood on the wall.

His ears fizzed, and a thousand ants crawled all over

his body. Wind swayed the branch with the ripe clementines above his head. He raised himself on his toes and reached for that branch.

He missed the branch and fell in the water.

The cold pierced his skin and sent a violent shock through him.

His heart throbbed to the point of bursting. He swam around the reservoir trying to find a foothold, but the water was too deep everywhere. He thrashed from one side to the other, scratched the concrete walls to reach the top, but the walls were too high for him to climb out.

He strived to remove his clothes and shoes, but he couldn't. He tried to scream, but the only sound that came out of his throat was a rasp. That too faded away as he kept on threshing from one end to another, trying to keep his body from freezing.

Then a clutch released within his ribs.

He stopped threshing. The side of his chest that thudded madly before had gone quiet suddenly.

He placed his hand over the heart—there was no beating anymore.

He looked up, gazed at the stars. The sky was lit with a dim white glow. In a few minutes, his senses would numb. Then he would sink into the deep unconsciousness and drift across the atomic barrier of life.

But, somehow, that didn't frighten him now.

He kept afloat with as little movement as possible. He waited for a sense of failure to seize him, but that feeling never came; instead, a sense of fulfillment embraced him all around. He had always stood up to life and never complained once. He had always given his best to the struggles and accepted with an even mind whatever came as results. He had always trusted the Universe for what was beyond his control.

He saw the fox. The animal now stood on the edge of the reservoir and looked keenly at him floating on the surface. Then François did something he had never done before. He brought his palms together on the chest and prayed:

"God, I've done all I could for Arthur. Please look after him now."

Then he saw himself on the wild coast of Brittany—as a toddler, in the arms of his father—learning to surf. The waves went roaring over them and crashed on the shore. His mother screamed in fear; but then, his father rose with a smile and lifted François in his arms.

And François let himself go.

Arthur finished revising for his exams then waited for his grandfather to return. Since he moved in with Grandfather, he had never gone alone to the church for supper. Recently, Grandfather had been coming home later and later into the evening, but, on the nights of meals at the church, he always returned before the soup kitchen closed.

Arthur knew Grandfather's battles with the publishers had intensified lately. Maybe, this evening, they were resolving their disputes finally, and he had to stay longer with them. It wasn't unusual for those who worked in Paris to return home as late as ten at night; Arthur had seen them descending from trains and rushing home with computers slinging over their shoulders.

Arthur looked at the watch. The soup kitchen would close in forty minutes, and, as usual, on the nights of meals at the church, there was nothing left in the fridge. There wouldn't be anything for two more days, if they missed this meal tonight. He had eaten a good lunch at school, but he needed to go to the church to collect food for Grandfather.

He knew Grandfather always lied about his meals outside home.

He knew that from the way Grandfather devoured those meals at the church. Arthur was worried how Grandfather's face looked so pale and bony these days, how the clothes hung loose over him, and how he panted and stooped while climbing stairs.

Lutetia too had seen him stopping at the benches when he walked through their town. Like Arthur, she was worried about his grandfather's falling weight. She even sneaked out fruits and yogurts for him from the canteen and gave them to Arthur. But Grandfather never touched those foods. Arthur had to eat them before they went bad.

Who knows, maybe tonight the two of them would have some good news to celebrate over dinner. In any case, Arthur couldn't let Grandfather skip a meal in his current frail state. He left a note on the kitchen table, pulled out the two food boxes they usually took with them to fill, and then went to the church.

The woman who served food stared at him oddly. But then, she smiled and filled his plate and the two boxes. He went to the people Grandfather sat with usually. They went silent for a moment, glanced at each other, then moved to make a place for him among them. They asked him questions about his day at the school and nodded along as he replied. He was proud to say that Grandfather couldn't come because he was busy signing the contract with a publisher in Paris, and that his new book would be out not before long.

On the way back from church, Arthur pondered how he could get a copy of the new book signed by Grandfather and give it to Lutetia. That would be a big surprise for her.

The note on the kitchen table was untouched. Arthur threw it in the garbage, took out a bowl from the cabinet, poured some soup into it, then put the rest of the food in the fridge. He pulled out the pieces of baguettes from his pocket and set them on the table next to the bowl.

He stood by the window.

He watched the trains from Paris. He searched among the people who came out, crossed the footbridge, and rushed to their homes. His mouth dried, his eyes itched. When he lived with his mother, she often left him alone at home late into the night, and he fell asleep worrying about her. But, next morning, when he woke up, she was always there.

This was the first time Grandfather was so late, though.

Why didn't he let Arthur know?

There was no way for him to reach Arthur.

Maybe Grandfather went out dining with his new publisher and forgot about Arthur.

No, that wasn't possible. He was forgetful these days, but not to that point.

Maybe he trusted Arthur to go to the church alone, and that's exactly what he had done. Now, on his part, he had to trust Grandfather too. The math and the physical sciences accounted for eighty percent of the grades; if he wanted to win the scholarship, he had to sleep well before the tests tomorrow. One more train came into the station. Grandfather didn't get down from it; certainly he would return later during the night.

Arthur drank a glass of water, changed into pajama, and went to bed.

As usual, he let himself fly to the stars, but the thoughts kept churning inside his head and forced him to turn from one side to another. Then he decided to stop those thoughts by revising his lessons in the head. Soon, he fell into the arms of sleep.

Next morning, he woke up with a throbbing pain behind his eyes.

In the kitchen, everything still lay on the table—exactly the way he had left them last night. A dull burning started in his chest. He didn't need to check, but he did anyway: Grandfather's bed hadn't been slept in last night. The burning grew sharper, and a panic started to take over him.

He opened the door of their apartment, checked the landing and the staircase. The woman from the floor above clacked down the stairs and went by him, barely smiling. People rarely talked to each other in this building. He heard the two neighbors behind their doors, but it had been ages since he last saw either of them. There was no point talking to them about Grandfather; they wouldn't know anything about him.

Where could Grandfather go?

He was not the type to leave Arthur behind and travel out of Paris. If he ever had to go away for long, he certainly would make all the arrangements for Arthur. Something must have happened to him. Arthur felt the air going out of his lungs. He rushed back into the apartment and closed the door.

But, what could happen to Grandfather?

Sure, he was not at the top of his form these days, but he was still smart. Nobody could mug him on the road or hurt him in the train. Mother owed money to people, but they wouldn't kidnap Grandfather to recover that money. Maybe he missed the last train from Paris, and his new publisher offered him a hotel for the night. He would return home before the end of the day. Arthur put the food in the fridge and left for school.

At school, he missed his tests altogether. He couldn't even read the questions.

At the canteen, he couldn't see what lay on his plate or hear what Thibault was saying. He kept seeing how, for two days, his mother lay on the bed, with her mouth open and her eyes half-closed; how he tried desperately to wake her up but couldn't move her limbs; how he poured water into her mouth and ended up drenching her bed. The images made him shudder. He rose from the table and carried his platter of untouched food to the counter.

Lutetia came over, frowning. She asked why he looked so fazed. Arthur said he had failed his tests. He didn't want to say anything about Grandfather; he feared evil omens might come upon him.

He sat through the afternoon classes, bent forward from his waist and bracing his arms over the abdomen. After school, he went to the park with his friends, just to keep those awful thoughts away from his head. Once his friends left, he wandered alone through the streets till late, and then turned toward home finally. He had denied his imaginations all day long, but now they showed him again what lay in wait inside their apartment.

When he reached home, he saw nothing like that.

Of course he had been stupid. No matter how difficult life was for Grandfather, he was not like Mother; he would never kill himself. Arthur showered, changed into fresh clothes, and sat at the kitchen table.

He didn't feel like eating. He started thinking what he should do.

At least, he wasn't locked inside the apartment, like he had been with Mother. He could go out and talk to Thibault or Lutetia. Thibault had his own problems at home, but Lutetia would help.

What could she do?

Call the police.

Arthur could do that himself.

But, he didn't want the police.

He had enough of them when they took him to the commissariat from Mother. Maybe Grandfather had to go to Brittany for some emergency in his family; he would return in a day or two. Arthur was big enough to stay alone in the apartment.

Fatigue dropped his eyelids. He went to his room and sat on the bed. Grandfather was a fighter—not one that died easily. God would never kill a great man like him. Arthur leaned back against the wall and closed his eyes.

There were knocks on the door.

Arthur sprang from the bed and almost fell to the floor.

There were voices on the landing outside, both familiar and unfamiliar, but none sounded like Grandfather's. Panic seized his guts again.

He tiptoed to the door and peeped through the bull's eye, but he couldn't make out the figures under the haze of the light bulb. He rubbed his eyes and looked again. There were four people on the landing, and all were looking intensely at this door.

Arthur stepped back and opened the door.

There were the two neighbors from his floor, a police officer with the hat in his hand, and a tall man with grey hair and goatee beard he had never seen before. A grave air hung around them.

"Hello, young man, I'm Bernard Dufour." The bearded man extended his hand. "A stubborn fan of your grandfather's books."

Arthur shook his hand. "Where is Grandfather?"

The man licked his lips and swallowed. "This afternoon, we found him—"

"That's our job, Monsieur Dufour." The police officer raised his hand. Then he took out a notepad and started reading out the details.

Arthur's legs gave away before the officer finished reading.

Madame Dufour crossed the bedroom, slid the floor-to-ceiling curtains aside, then glanced in the direction of Arthur. The morning sun, low in the sky, slanted through the glass panes and drew shapes of the bare branches over the wall. Arthur's head still felt soggy when he woke up, but his body wasn't so numb anymore. After a few hours in the park of their chateau, he could pull himself together again.

He had to. There was no other way.

Madam Dufour opened the glass door and stepped onto the balcony. The stripped poplars, covered with the fresh snow, stood like fireworks in white. Arthur sat up and wrapped the blanket around him. At the far end of the park, the branches of the clementine trees around the reservoir drooped under the weight of snow.

Arthur came out and stood next to Madame Dufour.

The cross and the wreath had gathered flakes too. At the base of the cross, where they first laid Grandfather, a group of ducks sat still.

Madame Dufour glanced at Arthur then placed her

hand on his shoulder. She didn't ask those questions again, and his eyes didn't burn this morning. For the first time in three weeks, he had slept through the night without any dreams. He still didn't know what would happen to him, but he had finally seen the place of Grandfather among the stars.

Arthur didn't want Grandfather to be alone.

"Mother!" Amelie called from the staircase. "Father is at the table."

Madame Dufour turned toward Arthur. "Do you want to go down now?"

Arthur nodded. He still didn't feel hungry that often, but these people never forced him to eat. And the silence they maintained when he sat quiet at the table didn't press down on him. Madame Dufour ran her fingers through his curls, then crossed the room and went down the stairs.

Amelie fidgeted around the door.

The girl had the usual sparkles in her eyes, but, this morning, there was a tinge of sadness he hadn't seen before.

Maybe her parents had received the decision about him from the judge finally. Maybe they would have to let him go to a State-owned orphanage. Maybe, that's why, Madame Dufour looked so grave and resigned this morning. He had started to love these people and their place, but, if he had to go to an orphanage, he would still continue to live. That was the least Arthur could do in return for the sacrifice Grandfather had made.

Life at orphanage didn't depress him anymore.

What depressed him now was the fate of Grandfather's new book.

He still had no idea how things finally turned out for Grandfather with the two publishers he had been dealing with. In the confusion that followed after his death, Arthur didn't even think of taking the manuscript with him. Now that apartment would go to Grandfather's relatives in Brittany; and, along with the rest of his belongings, the manuscript would go to them too.

From there, that manuscript would be lost for ever.

Amelie went down the stairs. Arthur dragged his feet through the bedroom and followed her.

Indeed, a change was there in the air of the living room. Monsieur Dufour sat with a document bearing official seals and scribbled notes on a pad. Those must be the papers from the court to send Arthur to the orphanage. Madame Dufour sat at his side and spread butter over the slices of baguettes.

"Sit down, young man." Monsieur Dufour said. "We have serious business to talk about this morning."

Madame Dufour kept her eyes on the table. Arthur went around and sat at his place before them. Amelie took the seat next to him and placed her hand on his wrist.

Monsieur Dufour stood up and walked to the armoire. He opened a drawer, pulled out a rectangular object wrapped in papers, and returned with it to the table. Amelie's grip tightened around Arthur's wrist.

Monsieur Dufour placed the wrapped object before Arthur. "This was the best we could do."

Amelie withdrew her hand, but Arthur's arm wouldn't move. He didn't want a gift from them before leaving.

"Open it, young man," Monsieur Dufour said.

Amelie lifted Arthur's hand and placed it on the gift.

His fingers shook, his lips trembled. He had a vague feeling what the gift might be, but it was too early for that. He bit his lip and looked away.

Monsieur Dufour unwrapped the gift and held it in his hands.

It was Grandfather!

He sat under a tree looking over a lake, but there was more.

A red fox stood nearby and observed something keenly. Arthur leaned forward to see what the animal was looking at, but his eyes had fogged already. He didn't know how to react to this portrait.

He lifted his head and looked around the table. The lips of Madame Dufour quivered, but Monsieur Dufour held his face firm. In Amelie's eyes, a strange light flickered in the pupils, sharpened by the wetness of the whites.

Arthur's nostrils itched. His eyes twitched a few times then went still. His face boiled, and his tongue became dry. The walls closed upon him.

"There is one thing I need to explain, Arthur," Monsieur Dufour said. "The fox is there on that portrait for a reason."

Arthur nodded.

"We found that fox floating next to your grandfather." He paused. "It seems the animal tried to save your grandfather from drowning."

Something shifted inside Arthur's chest.

He looked at Amelie. A stream of tears ran along each of her cheeks. He tried to inhale, but no air would go into his lungs.

Monsieur Dufour cleared his throat. "What I'm trying to tell you is this: your grandfather was *not* alone when he passed away from this earth."

Arthur sprang from his chair and darted to the corner of the room.

He hid his face there and sobbed. His chest quaked, his limbs shook. For the first time since Grandfather's death, Arthur finally let go and wailed. Madame Dufour came and held him in her arms. She rested her chin on his crown but didn't say a word.

They waited for Arthur to stop and take his seat. Then Monsieur Dufour looked up from the pile of papers; his eyes were red too.

"Real men cry to find their strength," he said. "Arthur has found his, for what he'll do this afternoon."

Arthur straightened his back and slid to the edge of his seat. He would sign the papers for the orphanage right now.

Monsieur Dufour slid the document with official seal toward Arthur. "You'll publish your grandfather's book."

"Me!"

"Yes. Take a look at that contract."

Arthur couldn't understand any of the legal terms, but he saw the book's title—and his name next to Grandfather's.

"But Grandfather said he couldn't publish this book because of an option clause."

"My lawyers have taken care of it already."

"Is this the new publisher's contract?"

"No. We're putting the manuscript on auction."

"What's auction?"

"You'll see. You'll be there this afternoon to close it."

Printed in Great Britain
by Amazon